domino

DOMINO BOOKS LIMITED

During the three minutes it took for Barney to make two orbits around his stomach, his stream of consciousness, expressed vocally only when he was in a reasonably upright position, resembled one of the darkest, most esoteric passages of *Finnegans Wake*...

'Ready to talk, Huggins?'

Barney's glasses had fallen off, but he could just about make out two seemingly enormous thighs towering up to a large black triangle. As he opened his mouth to speak, his teeth assumed that grotesque shape peculiar to people in upside down positions.

'I'm damned sure I am.'

THE TERROR OF HER WAYS

By
MIKE SHELLEY

The Terror of her Ways
is an original publication of Domino Books Ltd,
Edenderry Industrial Estate,
326/328 Crumlin Rd, Belfast BT14 7EE

© Mike Shelley 1984
ISBN 0 946963 02 9

Typeset, printed and bound in Northern Ireland by
Brough, Cox and Dunn Ltd, Clifton St, Belfast.
Set in 10 on 12 Century Textbook.

Cover and Design by Triplicate,
Linenhall St, Belfast
Illustration by Tony Bell

MAY 10   TORONTO

Jarvis Street isn't Toronto's skid row, but twice a day
the wino's and itinerants shuffle in from the beach and
the two blocks to the east, heading for the soup kitchens
of the Salvation Army and the Harbour Lights Mission.
Some of them occupy the derelict houses on the street,
building their days around bottles of cheap Canadian
sherry, until the Metro police come calling in their red
trousers, navy blue jackets and military-style peaked
hats.

At the station they are questioned about the latest
killing or beating inflicted upon one of their own kind,
given a multi-vitamin injection, advised to improve
themselves and stay clear of alcohol not intended for
human consumption, and then released. Most of the
policemen regard it as a pointless exercise, although they

may agree that it reduces the number of frozen bodies to be picked up during the severe Ontario winter.

Along with Yonge Street to the west and Sherbourne Street to the east, Jarvis is frequented by prostitutes; half a square mile known locally as the tenderloin area. The hookers on Yonge Street are mostly blacks from the U.S. Their day starts at 1.30 a.m. when the bars close and they take up their positions outside the all-night drug store.

Those on Jarvis Street are mostly white and not so nocturnal. They walk the street by day, waiting for a punter's car to pull up beside them, or sit alone at a table in the darkened bar of the Wiltshire Arms, listening to live Country music, and always waiting to be approached, never openly making the first move.

About one hundred yards from the Wiltshire Arms another building, even shabbier, stands half hidden behind three diseased elm trees. Only the two front rooms on the third and top floor have a good view of the street, and in one of them the grey net curtains had been slightly parted for almost two hours. It was 8:30 in the evening, the sun had gone down behind the commercial towers half a mile to the west, bestowing upon Jarvis a brief moment of radiance, and still the elderly grey-haired woman stood at the window surveying the pedestrians with her army-issue binoculars.

She had little interest in a tall blond man wearing a fawn suit who stopped below her and snapped a disposable lighter to his pipe. John Madrid — the name on his current Canadian passport — inhaled the mild tobacco like a cigarette. Smoke streamed from his nostrils as he resumed his stroll south along Jarvis Street towards the Wiltshire Arms.

For a few moments he stood at the entrance to the

bar, adjusting his eyes to the dimness. The lenses of his glasses were light sensitive, darkening in sunlight and only slightly tinted indoors. But that would be sufficient. He was unknown in the city. All of his 31 years had been spent in Montreal or London, England.

He sat at a table near the door. A two-piece group, organ and guitar, was playing 'Sea of Heartbreak' while a plump, smiling stripper went through her paces. The waiter brought him a beer and set up a fresh drink for the brunette at the next table. Madrid hadn't seen her signal for it, so he assumed she was one of the regulars, receiving automatic service. He leaned towards her and said softly:

'You working tonight?'

She looked at Madrid for a few seconds, appraising him, then lifted her glass and cigarettes and slid into the seat opposite him. As she did so, the sequins on her black costume sparkled faintly, and through the slit at the side he caught a glimpse of a firm shapely leg.

'What you got in mind?' she asked, staring at him.

'The usual.'

She reached for a cigarette. In one movement Madrid's lighter was out of his pocket and flaring in front of her face.

'Fifty bucks,' she said.

He nodded.

She sipped from her drink. Madrid glanced round the room once more. Two hookers were sitting on tall stools at the bar, talking to the bartender. The waiter was carrying a tray of drinks past the stage towards several groups of men sitting against the far wall, their faces and figures almost shrouded in the darkness.

'There's an hotel two blocks south of here,' she said. 'The Walbury. Check in under the name of Brown.

7

It'll cost you ten bucks. Wait for me in the room.'

'All right.' Madrid pocketed his pipe and stood up. The music had stopped. He glanced at the stripper now draped in a blue gown moving towards the bar; then he went out, leaving his beer untouched.

The brunette stared at the table, her cigarette burning in the tin ashtray. As the group started up again with 'Red Sails in the Sunset', a middle-aged man in gaudy checked pants and a windbreaker appeared in front of her.

'Okay if I sit with you?' he asked nervously.

The brunette shook her head.

'I'm waiting for a friend,' she said.

Madrid surveyed the room. Iron bed, two sheets, thin yellow blanket, side table, two hard-backed chairs and a washbasin with no soap. There was no telephone. He stood at the window and watched for the woman. Within five minutes he saw her tripping up to the entrance, her costume covered by a navy blue raincoat belted at the waist.

She knocked twice. He opened the door and stood back. She entered cautiously, looking around the room.

'Let's take care of the money first,' she said, after he had closed and locked the door.

'Sure.' He handed her two twenties and a ten. She moved towards the bed, unbuckling her coat. Even Madrid's keen eye had not spotted where she'd put the money.

'Where you from?' she asked.

'Toronto,' he said, pronouncing it *Trana* in the local fashion.

8

After slipping out of her costume she removed her bra and was about to pull down her black briefs when Madrid said:

'Leave those on for a while. I like them.'

A flicker of irritation crossed her face.

'All right, but this won't take that long.'

'I'll be quick,' promised Madrid, hanging his trousers over the back of the chair next to the bed.

She lay on top of the yellow blanket, her legs apart, hands covering her stomach. Even with customers she attempted to hide the spare tyre with its ugly stretch marks.

But Madrid seemed to like what he saw. As he knelt on the bed his eyes were fixed on the unusually large moons around her nipples. He bent over to kiss them, then brought his head back and, for the first time, smiled at her. She gave a weak smile in return and ran her hands down his strong back.

'What's your name?' he whispered.

'Kitty,' she said and dropped her hands over his buttocks, at the same time pulling down his Y-fronts a few inches.

'Not yet,' he said, grasping her wrists.

Releasing them, he kissed her breasts again then lowered himself so that he lay over her. As his left hand caressed her short fragrant hair, the other one moved slowly towards his jacket. Just before he forced the long stiletto blade under her ribcage, he placed his left hand firmly over her mouth and jaw.

After her silent scream had died away, he climbed off her and stood beside the bed. His face was expressionless as he plunged the knife into her eyes, cheeks, breasts, stomach and legs.

★ ★ ★ ★ ★ ★

Geoffrey Sides had trained to be an accountant, but like almost all of his life's endeavours he hadn't finished the course. He'd quit his last job as an internal auditor the previous July, ten days before his thirtieth birthday. For several weeks after that he wandered around the beaches near his home, a converted shop, on Queen Street East. As the fall came and winter approached, Geoffrey decided it was time to make use of the bank loan he had obtained, with great foresight, on the strength of his last job. Ostensibly for a European vacation, its real purpose was to set him up in his own business.

As it happened, Geoffrey was not an outstanding success as a small businessman. After making his living room into an office, he advised the commercial and industrial community of his availability as a consultant, a manfacturer's agent and a dealer in surplus commodities. The commercial and industrial community, with more wisdom than it realised, declined his offer. Geoffrey was reduced to placing ads in international magazines as follows:

'Young resourceful businessman will undertake assignments on your behalf or represent your company in Canada.'

Geoffrey had hoped that the word 'resourceful' would indicate to his prospective clients that he was not excessively finicky when it came to any inconvenient legal niceties. This, however, turned out to be insufficient inducement, for Geoffrey's only replies were from two Indians who wondered if the Esteemed Sir would be gracious enough to sponsor their entry into Canada. Since no mention was made of payment Geoffrey threw the letters into the waste basket.

After selling his office furniture and television, all of

which he had only rented, Geoffrey was further reduced to driving a taxi.

And it was Geoffrey Sides who was sitting in the orange cab outside the Walbury Hotel as John Madrid walked away from the mutilated body in the upstairs room.

Passing the lighted street lamp at the entrance, Madrid held his hand up to his face, as if to rub his nose. His glance into the taxi was met with a bespectacled stare from Geoffrey Sides, and it seemed to Madrid that the driver was taking more interest in him than was normal in a cabbie looking for a fare. Memorising the cab's number as he passed, Madrid walked north at a steady pace, his pulse and breathing normal, the images of his deed already fading from his mind. He turned left, towards the neon lights of the Yonge Street strip, and entered a car park to collect his rented Cutlass saloon.

Slowing down on Yonge for the Bloor Street lights, he was forced to brake sharply as a denim-clad youth ran from the sidewalk to avoid blows from a short pole being wielded by a stocky man with cropped black hair and large moustache. Standing between two cars, the agitated youth shouted 'Faggot!' and Madrid was reminded of Toronto's reputation as the San Francisco of the north, Canada's gay capital. The lights changed; as Madrid went through the intersection he glanced in his rear view mirror and was relieved to see the yellow police car he had spotted behind him stop beside the youth.

The traffic eased slightly as he continued north. After passing Lawrence Avenue he pulled into a 24 hours coffee shop. His mouth was dry and he wanted a smoke. It was an unsafe practice, he always thought, to fill a pipe while driving.

11

'Coffee, regular,' he ordered, placing forty cents on the counter. He carried his cup over to a table in the corner, and while the coffee cooled he brought out his straight-stemmed briar and pouch of aromatic tobacco.

His eyes followed the young waitress as she went around in a listless manner clearing the tables of cups and plates, her face showing neither intelligence nor the lack of it. He felt tired himself. He took a sip of the sweet coffee, still too hot, then looked up as the door opened.

The tinted glasses concealed his expression as he watched Geoffrey Sides walk up to the counter, glancing at both sides of the room, his hand digging for change in his jeans. After giving his order he pulled a pack of cigarettes from his shirt pocket, then got up on a stool. As the cab driver sat hunched over his coffee, Madrid stood up and strolled out, passing behind him on his way to the door.

After waiting for two women to climb into their car and leave the parking lot, he got out of his Cutlass and walked back towards the coffee shop. Then, shielded by a small truck, he ducked down and slid under the orange taxi.

At 11:30 Geoffrey Sides still had almost six hours to put in before his shift ended. Though he'd started at 6:30 he still hadn't earned the thirty dollars it cost him to hire the cab for the night; then there was the cost of gas on top of that. But trade usually improved after the bars closed, and by the time he'd seen the drunks home — with his tyre iron always close at hand — the subway had stopped running and he'd start to pick up the shift-workers, lovers and miscellaneous stragglers. Weekends were good too, with Friday and Saturday grossing more than the other four nights combined.

But all in all, it was a lousy way to make a living. Geoffrey didn't think he would be liable for any income tax this year, but even if he were he would contrive not to pay any. He was an accountant, after all, and as he liked to say with a self-deprecating smile, how many cab drivers are not drifters, gamblers and petty chisellers?

Cruising along Church Street he was flagged down by a dark-suited man with a briefcase.

'Airport. Think you can make it in under thirty minutes?'

'No problem this time of night,' said Geoffrey, thankful for a twenty dollar run, and headed north for Highway 401.

Meeting a pile-up on Avenue Road, he diverted onto Bathurst Street and went north on that, forgetting that the Bathurst access to the highway is for eastbound lanes only. The airport was west, so he had to go along to Dufferin Street, and by the time he was on the 401 the man in the back seat was showing signs of irritation.

'You been cab driving long?' he asked, and Geoffrey responded by stepping on the accelerator to move across two lines of traffic into the fast lane.

He was moving at 70 mph as he took the airport exit. There was no response from the brakes when he tried to slow down for the bend, so he pumped them. When that failed he jerked the automatic transmission into first gear and the cab shuddered and veered to the left. He swung the steering violently in the other direction, but the bend was upon them and the back of the cab swung onto the shoulder. The man in the back screamed as they toppled over the embankment, but Geoffrey just cradled his head in his hands and didn't make a sound.

★   ★   ★   ★   ★   ★

Her head on her chest, eyes closed, Catherine Deauville sat very still in the hard-backed chair by the window. The late morning sun streamed in through the net curtains at her back. A newspaper lay at her feet. Slowly she shifted upright and with an unsteady hand lit a cigarette, the smoke curling up through a shaft of sunlight to the ceiling. She reached down for the *Toronto Sun,* dated May 11, and started to reread the item halfway down page one.

HORRIFIC SLAYING IN JARVIS HOTEL

The grotesquely mutilated body of a woman was discovered last night in the Walbury Hotel. Cay Winterbrook, a 30 year old divorcee, was found dead in an upstairs room at 9:55 p.m. by an hotel employee. The woman, a regular patron of the hotel, had been seen going up to a room rented by a man at approximately 9:15. When she failed to reappear a search was made and the body found. Police are anxious to trace . . .

Catherine stopped reading, let the paper drop, and with an effort got to her feet. She stood at the window, seeing nothing but the imagined circumstances of her niece's murder. Her brother's wild, sad daughter. She didn't even know she'd been divorced. Tim probably didn't either. But then nobody told him anything anymore. She certainly hadn't let him know the real reason she'd come to Toronto from England — to locate Cay after a silence of two years.

After a while she began to think of her obligations in this matter — contact the police, identify the body. She didn't feel up to it; she was drained of energy, wanting only to leave this city and return to London.

But after coming this far she would have to see it through. Stirring herself, she pulled her suitcase from under the bed and started to pack. The binoculars she would leave for whoever wanted them.

Before phoning the police she picked up the *Toronto Sun* and placed it on top of her clothes in the suitcase. She had no interest in the other death report on page one:

CAB OVERTURNS ON 401. TWO DEAD.

Although it was 11:30 a.m. Lisa had been awake for less than fifteen minutes. Sitting at her Regency-style dressing table, brushing her short black hair, she could hear her maid preparing breakfast in the kitchen below. For a further twenty minutes she applied herself to her make-up — patting on the layers of moisturiser, foundation cream and blusher, peering into the small hand-held mirror as she dabbed on eye shadow and mascara, moving her lips together to smooth out the red gloss, and brushing the dark red polish onto her manicured finger nails. When she had finished she looked remarkably younger than her 43 years.

As 12 struck from the small church at the end of her Kensington mews, she stood up and slipped out of her green satin dressing gown. Naked, she walked over to a built-in cupboard unit, her feet touching pleasantly on the plush carpet. From a drawer she removed a bra, a garter belt, nylon briefs and a pair of seamed nylons — all of them, except the stockings, of the same shade of black. Lisa was getting ready for work.

She had entered into her underwear and was reaching for the dressing gown when her private phone rang. She stepped over to the bedside table and picked up the receiver.

'Yes.'

'Madrid here.'

'Go ahead.'

'It went okay. No problems.'

'Where are you now?'

'I'm still over here. I'll be back in four or five days.'

'Why so long?'

'Should be obvious. Toronto airport's not suitable, so I'm heading south and making a detour from there.'

'You're sure that's the only reason?'

'Look, don't crowd me, all right? It went okay, that's all you need to know.'

'Very well.' Lisa replaced the receiver and went down for her breakfast.

Two days later Lisa sat at the kitchen table smoking a cigarette. She sipped at her tea and considered the preferences of her next client.

I wonder why he no longer wants the German governess, she thought smiling. I must have put him off that routine. He probably thought it came a little too near the bone. She snorted in contempt. Can't keep away though, can he? The way he keeps coming back, you'd think he lived for the damned thing.

Hearing her maid's plodding steps in the hall, she smiled again, anticipating the denouement of the next session. The elderly woman looked in and said:

''E's arrived. I've put 'im in the back room.'

'All right.' She poured another cup of tea. Another five minutes, she thought. They like to wait. Even they know it's the wrapping that's important, not the product.

Milton Wilmar was sitting naked as she made her grand entrance into the back room, her full-length negligee allowing tantalising glimpses of her underwear. He stood up promptly and reached her the money, £70 plus £5 for the maid. She snapped it from his hand, counted it expertly, then pointed a slender finger at the chair in the corner.

'Look how you've left your clothes,' she said sharply. 'Just look at them! They're a disgrace! I want you to get over there and fold them *properly*.'

For several minutes she stood over him, arms akimbo, repeatedly making him re-arrange the clothes, rewarding his futile efforts with sharp tugs of his ear and slaps across the face.

'You stupid dog!' she shouted, affecting a rage. 'You're getting worse instead of better. You know what this means, don't you?'

He nodded. She slapped him across the ear.

'Answer me properly,' she shouted into his face. 'What does this mean?'

'It means the cane, mistress.'

'Yes, it does. Now crawl over there and bring me the most evil cane in that cabinet. And I mean the most *evil* one.'

After receiving ten minutes more physical and

18

verbal abuse over his repeated failure to return with the most evil cane in the collection, Wilmar was made to bend over a chair and count the strokes while Lisa administered one of the beatings that he craved so much beforehand but always found intensely painful at the time.

The session reached its crescendo with Wilmar on the rack and Lisa alternately teasing and hurting with a multi-thronged tawse. As she released him from the leather straps, she smiled and said:

'Take a shower, Milton, then come into the sitting room for a drink. I need your help again.'

Swearing fluently under his breath, Milton Wilmar, a senior official in the Department of Defence, waddled over to the waste-paper bin and dropped in the bulging condom.

Milton Wilmar thought it was a bit thick. Getting blackmailed by tarts for money was one thing, but when they demanded confidential Ministry documents — well, that was quite another. It just wasn't on. No, this was definitely the last time. If she asked again he'd tell her to go to blazes. Let her cause a scandal. Men of his position and background rarely went to prison, and with almost a quarter of a million in property and investments he certainly had enough to tide him over until the eventual return to grace.

Then there was the wife. No point in hoping that she'd even begin to grasp the fact that he'd done it purely to protect her and the boys. Seeing his point of view had never been one of Laura's strong points, he was sorry to say.

Wilmar stopped pacing his office and returned to his upholstered chair. He lit another cigarette from the first packet he'd bought in over a year; the butt of the previous one still smouldered in the large marble ashtray. Even the shock of Lisa's first demand a month earlier had not caused him to start smoking again. 'Just this once, Milton dear,' she'd said, her brown eyes looking frankly at him, 'and I'll never ask you for anything again.'

He hadn't enquired why a London callgirl should want to peruse secret War Office files on the British advance into Germany in 1945 — all that stuff was old hat now anyway — and sitting with a scotch in his hand within the aura of the beautiful woman who had had for most of the previous hour almost total control over him, he didn't see much harm in doing as she asked. But now she had broken her word, given, he might add, to a very senior official in her Majesty's Civil Service, and he, Milton Wilmar, did not propose that she should do that with impunity. He reached for the phone.

'Diane, do I have any appointments this afternoon?'

'Just one, sir,' his personal assistant informed him. '2:30. With Mr. Johnston and Mr. Reeves.'

'Yes, that's it. Give them a ring, will you? Tell them I've been called away on urgent business. Reschedule for tomorrow at the same time. I should be back before four o'clock.'

Wilmar felt strangely excited as he left his office. He was about to do something he'd never done before.

Returning from this third visit to the WC at the end of the corridor since his lunchtime refreshments, Barney

Huggins wondered why he had been so dilatory in replacing the stick-on letter E that had been pulled off the smoked glass top of his office door by a person or persons unknown.

'Always create the right impression' had been perhaps the commonest, but by no means the vaguest, of the nuggets of advice he liked to hand out, accompanied by a knowing smile that didn't sit quite right on his battered, bespectacled features, to his admirers down at the Bunch of Grapes. And yet here he was, trying to make a go of his second most interesting enterprise ever — the first was flogging British Army stores to the natives during the Korean War — and he had to do it behind a door that informed prospective clients and other passersby that he was a PRIVAT DETECTIVE.

Shaking his head, he crossed the polished wooden floor to the oak desk that dominated the room, his gait — the four lunchtime pints notwithstanding — as stiffly erect as ever. He would, he had decided in the five steps it took to cross the office: (a) definitely do something about that sign, and (b) refuse point blank to allow himself to be further intimidated by unreasonable creditors. Besides, once you're on the bad payers list, he thought almost happily, you don't have to worry any more about losing your credit rating.

At 3:10, after two dunning phone calls, Barney was wondering whether it would not be better if he were to remove himself from both his business and private addresses until such time as he and his creditors could put things in a clearer perspective. When, at this point, the office door opened and a heavy-set man stepped in, Barney's reaction was a confused medley of (a) disposing of the latest issue of *Sophisticated Sex Life*, (b)

21

wondering what company this man represented, and thus which of his current excuses was applicable, and (c) cursing his bad luck that Big Max should finally send in the enforcer just as he, Barney, had definitely decided to vacate all his premises and haunts.

When Barney's practised eye did get around to focusing on the entrant, he noted the fine cut of his Savile Row suit and above that the fat, sleek jowls that hung from a face totally devoid of the steely stare he had come to expect in his visitors, and he deduced from his observations that he had nothing at all to fear from this man.

'Mr. Huggins?' asked Milton Wilmar, approaching the desk.

'And your name, sir?' replied Barney, habitually non-committal, his Belfast accent still discernible after more than thirty years in England and abroad.

'Mundle. Antony Mundle,' said Wilmar, having selected the name of the chap for whom he had fagged during his public school days. 'Are you free to take on a . . . a case, Mr. Huggins?' Wilmar was almost enjoying himself.

'Sit yourself down, Mr. Mumble.' Barney indicated a hard-backed chair next to the hat stand.

'Mundle's the name, actually.'

'Precisely,' said Barney, staring at him through his hornrimmed spectacles as if he had just hit upon the clue that destroyed Wilmar's masquerade, effortlessly exposing him as a vile and infamous traitor. Wilmar shifted uneasily in his seat — as well he might since the chairs Barney provided for his visitors were singularly uncomfortable.

'As it happens, you're in luck,' announced Barney. 'I've just completed the first phase of a tricky case . . .

And now I'm free for a limited period,' he added with more truth than he realised.

'Ah, good.' Wilmar produced his packet of Players, and Barney took the opportunity to snap open his silver cigarette case, a souvenir of his first assignment, and light up one of the bulging handrolled that represented the total of his morning's work.

'I have in fact,' continued Wilmar,' a rather delicate and complex problem —'

'No job too difficult, that's my motto, Mr. Mundle,' said Barney reassuringly.

At this point Wilmar was re-evaluating his decision to employ the services of an investigator of this calibre and B.H. Huggins in particular. He had decided against going to one of the large reputable agencies — there was a danger there of more being revealed than he could stand — and opted instead for the down-market type who, as long as the money was there, felt quite happy being lied to. An individual who could be fooled and, if necessary, intimidated. Wilmar decided to continue with Barney Huggins.

'To be quite frank about it,' he said, taking the nettle firmly in hand, 'I'm being blackmailed by a callgirl.'

After suppressing a snigger, Barney nodded his understanding.

'Carry on.'

'I was wondering whether or not you could investigate her with the purposes of . . . ' He gestured in the air.

'Dig up the dirt on her, you mean?'

'Well . . . yes.' Wilmar seemed reluctant to agree with this definition of the enquiry. 'What I would like is certain information that would enable me to . . . '

'To exchange the old *quid pro quo's*,' put in Barney,

always relishing the opportunity to use one of his four Latin phrases; the others being *ignotum per ignotius, suspendatur per collum,* and *in flagrante delicto.*

'If you like,' said Wilmar, and proceeded to prime Barney Huggins with as much misinformation and facts as were necessary for the detective to embark upon his investigation.

On the morning of May 16 Catherine Deauville arrived at Heathrow in the economy section of a British Airways 747. Her legs were cramped after the restrictions of the seven hour flight and the six gins taken on an empty stomach had left her with a nauseous headache. She hadn't slept since her niece's funeral almost two days before. A short, perfunctory ceremony with only nine mourners, eight of them women.

Tim had been unwilling to attend. His daughter, he'd stated during her second phone call, was to be cremated at his expense. He was very sorry about what happened, of course, but he felt it would be pointless for him to fly four thousand miles to pay respects to a corpse. Although they had been deeply estranged for several years, he would honour Cay's memory in his own way. He reminded Catherine that he'd had Diana, his first wife, cremated too; so there was no judgement involved in choosing that method for Cay.

Catherine had a porter convey her case to the stand for the Victoria bus. She'd take a taxi from Victoria station to her flat in Holland Park, she decided; it was too expensive hiring one all the way from Heathrow.

After buying her ticket she sat on a bench and waited for the bus to arrive. Within a minute she heard her name being called and looked up to see the slim figure of her younger sister, Mary, hurrying towards her.

'Sorry I'm late, dear. Got caught in a jam. But why are you sitting out here? I told you I'd meet you. Been looking everywhere in there and then I thought ... Oh, isn't it terrible about Cay? You look absolutely all-in. Now, come on, we'll scoot back to your flat and pick up your things. Then you're going to spend a day or two with me. I was so worried about you. No, I insist. Let me take that bag.'

Catherine made her wait while she went up to the booth and asked for a refund on her unused ticket.

The following afternoon in Lisa's baroque sitting room John Madrid, newly arrived from Los Angeles, was informing her of the slight hitch that marred the operation in Toronto.

'Gave himself away outside the hotel. Stared right at me like he was trying to know me again. But I wasn't too worried. I had my shades on and it was dark. Come to that, the hotel desk clerk and maybe somebody in the bar would have had a much better look. But then he followed me into this all-nighter — short guy with glasses he was — and I couldn't risk it further than that. I read next day he'd totalled his cab on the highway. Him and this passenger who was with him, they both bought it.'

Lisa placed her glass of chilled white wine on a delicately fashioned coffee table and stood up. As Madrid watched her walk past him — her feline, languid movement, the sway of her backside under the snug blue dress — he experienced a surge in his groin that he did not find entirely welcome. It might be costly, he thought, to relax his guard with this beautiful but unpredictable woman.

She seemed preoccupied. Leaning against the fireplace, she regarded him with dark, made-up eyes. At length she said:

'That is none of my concern.'

'What isn't?'

'The driver of the taxi isn't.'

Before answering he snapped on his lighter and held it to the bowl of his pipe, puffing up a small cloud of aromatic smoke. *The driver of the taxi isn't.* That's an awkward way of saying it, he thought, doubting once more her claim to have been born in South Africa.

'Oh, sure,' he said. 'That one's on my account.' Rising from his chair, he walked over to where she was standing. He stood with his head so close to hers that he could smell the natural fragrance of her hair.

'I want to get this over with as soon as possible,' he said softly.

'So do I,' she said, moving a step away from him. 'But it must be done right. I have waited too long to rush it now.'

'You're the boss. So who's the next one?'

'Another woman. I'll get you the details now.'

As Madrid was transcribing her handwritten note, Lisa stood at the window, looking down at the street.

'Please come over here a moment,' she said, and when Madrid was beside her she pointed a manicured finger at a stocky man wearing spectacles and a hat who was standing on the other side of the road.

'He was down there last night and again this morning. Look after him, will you?'

★ ★ ★ ★ ★ ★

Catherine Deauville strolled along the bank of the small river near her sister's house on the outskirts of Luton. It was warm for May, almost seventy degrees, and she'd taken off the top of her brown woollen suit, carrying it sedately over her arm. After an hour's walking in the sun her armpits were wet and sticky, though glancing down at the front of her cotton blouse she could see no stains on the white fabric. She would take a shower when she got back, she thought, and change into a cool dress for dinner. Mary was preparing lobster and salad, followed by a creme caramel. She decided to call in to the wine shop on the way back and surprise her with a top-notch white wine — Chablis perhaps — which would make a change from the Italian red they'd had last night and from the Portuguese whites Catherine bought for herself each weekend in London. Mary and Sam had been very kind to her these past two days.

As she stopped to take out her handkerchief there was a flash of blue and green that streaked across the water from one bank to the other, and Catherine felt a small thrill of pleasure at this sighting of the elusive kingfisher. Unusually for a woman who'd spent most of her life in London, she had always been a keen ornithologist. Her weekends in the west country and occasionally the Scottish highlands had brought her into contact with many nice, sensitive men, with only a few of them, contrary to the public notion of birdwatchers, even slightly eccentric. They did tend to be married though; but that was an irritation of the past: at 61 Catherine had long since accepted and made the best of her single life.

Newly retired after thirty five years in the bank, she would find enough contentment in indulging her passion for Mozart and Bach, catching up on her reading in three

27

languages — she had attended advanced French and German courses at night school in the fifties, enjoying a quiet extra-curricular relationship with her instructor, a balding bachelor approaching middle-age — and, of course, pursuing her interest in the wild birds of Britain, particularly the crow family, in which she specialised. Not the most fashionable species, by any means, but she'd always found them to be the most amusing and intelligent of birds. Perhaps she'd discover a new nesting site for ravens, or even the red-legged choughs. Now that would be divine.

By the time she'd completed her walk and called in at the wine shop it was almost 4:30. Wearing her jacket now and clutching a bag with the bottle of Chablis — it was surprisingly expensive, something to do with the falling pound, she supposed — she hurried along the high street to the bus stop. Mary's estate was only four miles out, so she'd be there shortly after five. That would give her time to shower and change and then give Mary a hand with some little chore like setting the table.

She was glad Mary and Sam believed in having dinner at a sensible hour — not like some of the people she'd stayed with who disrupted the whole evening by waiting until eight or even nine before sitting down to a long, alcoholic dinner. She smiled as a line from a once-popular song flowed through her head: 'She gets too hungry for dinner at eight.' Then her light-heartedness abruptly faded as she recalled the title. Tim had used that very word in one of his rages against the absent Cay; indeed, it was one of his milder terms of abuse. With an annoyed shake of the head she banished the melody of 'The Lady is a Tramp' from her mind.

By the time the bus arrived she had regained her equanimity. She'd done her best for Cay, even to the extent of seriously depleting her savings in an attempt to locate her; but now the girl was dead and she didn't propose to let the horror of her death haunt the remaining years of her own life. A hard, unfeeling attitude perhaps, but one she felt she must attempt to adopt in order to regain her peace of mind, her capacity to enjoy life. As the bus moved through the rush hour traffic Catherine turned her thoughts to the coming week in London: the concert at the Albert Hall with Bach's St. Matthew Passion, a day exploring the second-hand bookshops, the weekly visit by her friend Doris when they'd share a bottle of sherry and talk about literature and music until 11 p.m.

Climbing the hill from the bus stop she anticipated Mary's surprise at her little gift, her gentle scolding for being extravagant, and then Sam's pleasure when he arrived tired and hot from the office and saw the Chablis cooling in the ice bucket.

After letting herself in she hung up her jacket on the coat stand in the hall. There was the sound of classical music — Mahler, she thought — from the radiogram in the living room, and as she opened the door she called, 'I'm back.'

She sat down on the settee and slipped gratefully out of her suede shoes. She'd bought them specially for going to Canada and they were still a little too new for doing a lot of walking in. But then the pleasantness of the river and the fine weather had seduced her into staying out longer than she'd intended. She sighed with relief as she rubbed the soreness out of her cramped feet.

'Mary, I'm back,' she called again.

Yes, that was Mahler, she decided. She recognised his style, but for the life of her she couldn't identify the piece. Doris would know straight away, she thought smiling. She was talking about him and buying recordings of his works long before he came into fashion. Same with that English writer, Tolken or Tolkein. Mary mentioned him too, last year sometime. Mary was surprised at her ignorance of his works. It was almost a cult, she'd said, particularly among younger people. Catherine's response had been a quibbling enquiry about who else but the young were attracted to cults, but she promised all the same to look out for his books and read at least one of them. She hoped her sister wouldn't remember that.

The chiming of 5:30 from the grandfather clock in the hall prompted Catherine to get up and see what Mary was doing. She went over in her stockinged feet to the kitchen door and opened it, her mouth already half open to say hello. Then she screamed at the bulging, distorted features of her sister as she hung by the neck from the ceiling, her body still gently swaying.

Sitting at his desk Barney Huggins considered his next move in a most promising case. The first phase of his undercover investigation had revealed that the subject was being visited by men on a frequent and regular basis. He wasn't sure that Mr. Mundle would be entirely happy parting with £50 per diem plus expenses for the two days it took to gather that intelligence, but Barney was nevertheless enormously pleased with his progress. He had always maintained that 'information means money', and now that he had several photographs of prosperous-looking men emerging from a callgirl's apartment he felt better informed than he had been for ages.

The butt that had sat lifeless in the corner of his mouth for the past ten minutes crept up his cheek as he smiled in contempt at the pathetic precautions four of them had taken in parking their cars in the next street. It was the work of mere moments for a professional to saunter after them and jot down the licence numbers. Two of them, he was pleased to note, drove cars that indicated substantial reserves of wealth.

The first phase, although rewarding, had been very boring. Also, there was a limit to the amount of cover that could be obtained from posing as a pedestrian or a man tying his shoelace or, traffic wardens permitting, a driver sitting in a parked car. The next stage, however, promised to be much more entertaining, and for that he proposed — just on the off chance he had been spotted in the street — to make use of his disguises.

He pulled out the large drawer of his desk and from the back of the immaculately maintained files of unprocessed bills produced a thick brown moustache. Using the silver cigarette case as a mirror, he had just positioned it under the battered mass of broken capillaries that constituted his nose when the door opened and a man wearing a well-cut beige suit and a hat stepped in.

'B.H. Huggins?' he said, pushing the door closed behind him.

Barney, noting that the ominous steely glint was very much in evidence in the eyes of this ugly-looking customer, decided on the spur of a particularly anxious moment to go undercover.

'I'm waiting for him myself,' he said, and noting a fleeting trace of confusion in the man's steely glint, wondered at himself for not hitting upon disguises before as a device to confound his creditors. 'Can I give him a message?'

The man nodded. 'Tell him I've got a job for him.'

'An investigation, you mean?' Barney's cover was taking a new and more concrete form.

'What else?'

'Well, I should have mentioned earlier that I'm Mr. Huggins' partner. He's away on an important case at the moment, so I'm handling the rest of the agency's business. Take a seat and I'll see what I can do for you.'

The man walked over from the door and sat down in the chair by the hat stand.

'This is a very confidential matter,' he said flatly.

Barney held up a reassuring hand.

'This is the most discreet agency in the business. In fact, it's our speciality.' About to embark on an horrific tale of his partner suffering jail and police brutality rather than disclose the identity of a client, he thought better of it and contented himself with a nod and an arch smile. 'So don't worry if it's a bit ... you know ...'

The man stared at him, his features expressionless.

'I get the idea,' he said.

'So that's all right.' Barney adopted a businesslike manner. 'Now, what's the problem?'

'Tomorrow night a merchant ship will put in at London docks. After customs have been cleared, a black crewman will come off that ship and he'll be looking for me. I'd like you to meet that man and take him to a certain address in St. Pancras.'

'Why can't you meet him yourself?'

'I have business elsewhere.'

'Why's it so confidential?'

'Because there are political enemies after him.'

'A crewman?'

'He's incognito.'

A likely story, thought Barney, who had strongly developed instincts about this sort of thing. He considered the matter for a while then slowly nodded his acceptance. He didn't believe a word of what he'd just been told but he hadn't turned down a case yet, and for this one he'd insist on full payment in advance.

'You'd better give me the details,' he said, opening his stationery drawer for a clean sheet of paper. 'Though it seems fairly straightforward.'

'There should be no problem with this one,' said the man in the hat and beige suit, reaching for his pipe and disposable lighter.

MAY 20   HALFIELD

His sister's death had come at a very inconvenient time
for Tim Deauville. Sitting at his desk in the Halfield
speciality steel works, he ground the point of his pencil
through several sheets of a pad of blank transfer slips.
Around him in the open-plan office four other clerks were
engaged in various calculations regarding the purchase
and use of raw materials, the most important of which
being the iron scrap that was bought in large quantities
from numerous Black Country dealers. It was stored in
huge piles at the north of the plant before being moved
by rail car into the two furnaces that transformed it into
a glowing, molten mass of almost pure iron. It was one
of Tim's jobs to enter daily purchases and usage onto the
Kardex system which recorded the current inventories
of the iron scrap.

Tim couldn't possibly risk going down to Luton tomorrow for Mary's interment; but what reason could he give for not being there? He could hardly say it was because the auditors were in, that they'd be concluding their review of his section within the next day or two, and it was important that as chief clerk he be there. That was true enough, they *were* in, four polite bastards in three-piece suits, smiling and nodding and superficially anxious that they were not disturbing him, yet quick to remind him with a glance or change in tone of their power, of the iron fist under the velvet glove. But he could not use their presence as an excuse for not attending the funeral tomorrow, any more than he could have used it for avoiding the trip to Toronto. If only Sam and Catherine could realise how vital it was that he remain here until the auditors leave. Even one day's absence could be disastrous.

'You coming?' asked Albert from the next desk, one of Tim's two subordinates. 'The snoops left ten minutes ago. Saw them file out clutching their little black bags when I was down at reception.'

Tim glanced at his watch. It was 4:58. Their early departure was a good sign, he felt. It meant that they thought there was nothing big or urgent left to be completed. Of course, they might be coming back later after everyone had gone.

'Yes, I think I will have an early night,' he said and started to tidy his desk. He busied himself with this until Albert and the other clerks had gone, then he locked his drawers and reached for the phone.

Leaving the company car park in his 75 Cortina Tim turned right towards the town centre. His home — a surburban semi-detached — lay in the other direction, but tonight of all nights Tim needed the balm of Wendy's company.

He didn't usually see her on Wednesday evenings: they had agreed at the beginning that it would be better to fix set times for his visits. That way, she had said, they could organise their other lives around their relationship. Tim had objected that it meant their affair was organised too, and he wasn't at all sure that he wanted her to have 'an other life'. But he had to agree; it was only logical to regulate their arrangement, one that he had himself instituted when, on their second meeting, he persuaded her not to leave Halfield for London, clinching it with an offer of a rent-free flat in the most fashionable part of town. For the first month she retained her job at the cosmetics counter in a local department store, but after leaving that — some unpleasantness with the manager — she began to talk once more of moving to London, and so he was forced to give her an allowance. Although she would be the last to admit it, Wendy was a kept woman.

One thing he had insisted on, though, was a key to the flat, and as he opened the panelled door he felt uneasy about not being able to notify her of his arrival. He had tried to phone her from the office, but there was no answer, and he was sure Wendy would not be mollified by that inadequate attempt. She tended to react harshly to invasions of her privacy, even by the man who, in a sense, provided it. Yet that hadn't deterred him; listening to the phone ring repeatedly in her bedroom had only increased his desire for her, the sound itself tantalising him by its presence in that room.

'Wendy,' he called. When there was no response he went through the living room with its ferns and light pastel colours, and into the bathroom.

He stood under the shower for ten minutes, turning up the needle-point jets until the heat and force of the water on his slim frame was just past the point of comfort. After washing his hair and moustache, still glossy black at the age of 55, he stepped out onto the white tiled floor and rubbed himself briskly with a fresh towel. Then, in anticipation of the evening's lovemaking, he opened the medicine chest for his razor and shaving brush. He usually kept them at the top left corner, behind the tin of talc, but he was only slightly irritated when he found they weren't in the chest. Feeling relaxed after his shower, he smiled at the compulsion women felt every now and again to move things from one place to an obscurely more suitable one.

After dressing he went into the living room and opened the cocktail cabinet. He poured two inches of gin into a highball glass then filled it with white lemonade and ice. That first drink after work should be strong and chilling, but Wendy could never remember to store the mixes in the fridge, as he had suggested, and she'd laughed outright when he asked her to keep his gin there too.

Leaving his drink to cool through for a few minutes, he went into the bedroom and picked up the phone. It was after 5:45; his wife would be home from her office by now.

'Yes, it's me. I'm at the plant ... That's right, they're still here. We'll be out in the yard for an hour or two, rechecking the stocks. You know what they're like ... No, I can't say. You make something to eat for yourself ... Well, it'll be all over in a day or two. See you later.'

Returning to the living room, he sat on the settee and sipped from his drink. The first one usually affected his legs first, a glowing lightness that spread upwards, remained for several minutes, and then faded away; a gentle rush that the second drink, even after a few hours delay, could never seem to duplicate. He was mixing that second gin when he heard a key in the door.

'Hello, darling. I did try to phone you.'

Wendy made no effort to disguise her irritation. 'What brings you here tonight?' She closed the door firmly and threw her handbag on the settee.

'To see you, of course.'

'Yes, but you know Wednesday's not one of your nights. That's what I'm saying.'

'You needn't be so hostile. Have I done something wrong?'

She sighed in exasperation.

'No, you haven't done anything *wrong*. It's just that tonight is my night for . . . Oh, forget it.'

'For what, darling?' he asked casually as she strode past him.

Turning at the bedroom door, she said:

'For any bloody thing I like. I thought that had been made clear at the start.'

The door slammed.

He sat on the settee, bent over, his drink on his lap, sipping from it. He had expected her to be irritated, but not irate and harsh like this. What was she doing in there? He'd go in and talk to her when she'd had time to cool down. He felt hurt, but not angry. As he thought about her harshness his need to be comforted by her grew greater. On top of everything else he needed to heal their relationship, win back the affection of the woman for whom he had risked so much.

He put down his empty glass and went over to the bedroom door. There were the faint tones of a piano concerto from the radio inside and above that the sound of her talking on the phone. He pressed his ear against the wood, but her voice was indistinct. At the sound of the receiver being put down he opened the door and stepped just inside. Her eyes flashed up at him.

'Would you like a drink?' he said.

She shrugged.

'Make it scotch and ice.'

When he returned with the drink she was stepping out of her light-coloured paisley dress. Letting it drop to the carpet, she walked past him to the dressing table and sat down on the stool. He set the glass beside her and stood watching her brush her long auburn hair. Each stroke seemed to absorb him: the sweep of her hand, the lustre like burnished copper that seemed to increase with each dip of the blue nylon brush, the rising of the light, cracked hairs after each stroke, and the way the ends danced on her skin below the strap of the bra. At last he said:

'I was entirely in the wrong, you know.'

Her face looked up at him in the mirror. She smiled. She put down the brush and sipped at her drink.

'Of course you were, darling.'

'It won't happen again.'

'I wouldn't have minded so much if you'd rung me during the afternoon.'

'Well, this is it.'

'I mean, I might have been bringing my mother home with me. What would she have thought to find a strange man in the flat?'

'Or your father,' he added playfully. She'd never mentioned her parents, but he knew they were living abroad at some Forces base.

She smiled as their eyes met in the mirror.

And you are a strange man, aren't you, darling?'

He moved forward and placed his hands on her shoulder.

'No, but I am crazy,' he whispered, grasping her firm, young breasts. 'Just crazy enough to go out and buy you the car you've been hinting about. I was looking at a 79 MG today.'

'Oh darling!' Her use of the word was no longer ironic.

His sexual urge intensified by the impulsive promise, he tightened his grip on her breasts and kissed her passionately on the neck and shoulders. The inspiration came suddenly. He said:

'That's what I came to tell you tonight.'

'But you should have said!' Pulling his hands away, she rose from the stool and placed her arms around his neck. She kissed him long and hard, her breath fragrant with whisky, her tongue exploring his mouth. Her hand slipped down and grasped his bulging crotch.

'Let's do something with that,' she said, her mouth against his. She smiled as his hands moved up from her buttocks and began to pull down her tights.

He lay on the bed with her kneeling over him, sitting on his thighs. She bent forward to kiss him and he turned his head so that she would thrust her tongue into his ear. Then she ran the flat of her tongue up his face, over his eyes, and he could feel the texture of it, hot and moist, on his skin. She sat back and started a gentle rock. He closed his eyes, his mind a pleasurable haze. As her rhythm became more intense, the door bell chimed, shattering his mood. She stopped and remained quite still. The chimes came again.

'Don't answer it,' he whispered.

Still joined, they listened as the bell sounded

insistently, a finger kept on the button. She raised herself from him.

'Please don't answer it,' he said.

She put on a dressing gown and went out, closing the bedroom door after her. He moved quietly to the door and opened it an inch.

'Sorry to bother you, miss. Is your name Wendy Staston?'

'Yes.'

'Detective-sergeant Matthews. May I come in and ask you one or two questions?'

'Certainly.'

His voice came nearer.

'Are you acquainted with Wesley Thomas Calton of 21 Damien Gardens, Halfield?'

'What's this about?'

'Please answer the question, miss. It is important.'

'Yes, I do know him.'

'When did you see him last?'

A pause.

'Last night.'

'During what time?'

Her voice was faint but it struck him with the impact of a shout.

'All last night.'

'Please specify the times, miss.'

'From about ten to eight this morning.'

'Was he out of your sight at any time?'

'No.'

'And where were you during this period?'

'At his house.'

'21 Damien Gardens?'

'Yes.'

'Thank you, miss. You've been most helpful.'

A sound of steps on the carpet.

'Have you arrested him?'

'Why should we do that, miss?'

'No reason that I know of. But you should tell me something about this. Is he . . . is he helping you with your enquiries?'

'Yes, miss, he is. Goodnight.'

Tim was feeling very faint; the thump of his heart came fast and loud in his ears. He lay down on the bed. Why now? Why did that fool Calton have to get himself pulled in now? Damn him! He swore he'd finished with that other stuff. Or is it . . . Oh God, don't let it have anything to do with the plant.

As he lay on his side clutching the pillow, Tim's other shock came over him once more; a surge of rage and hurt that seemed to make the blood rush to his head. He wanted to storm out there, grab her by the hair and send his hand crashing onto her pretty face until she was swollen and bleeding. He wanted to stand over her naked, bloody body and hurl down obscenities with all the venom at his command. He wanted to pick up a hatchet and smash every stick of the psuedo-Californian furniture, terrorising her as the vicious blows of his axe came inexorably nearer to her cringing, moaning form. He wanted to run out with a new ferocious mind and track down Calton, battering and stomping him until he whined for mercy.

But he knew he was in much too precarious a position for a display of heroics of that sort. His rage was quickly displaced by a feeling of intense despair. The hurts and shocks of the past ten days seemed to eat away at his vitals. He wondered how a man could be expected to bear so much in such a short time. His daughter, his sister, the auditors, Wendy, Calton. Surely nothing more could happen to him now. He crawled up into a fetal position and clutched the pillow against his face. He began to cry.

MAY 20   LONDON

Barney Huggins hadn't meant to start off quite so late for his assignment down at the docks, but his landlord had taken the outrageous — and illegal — step of sending along three workmen to change the lock in Barney's office door. It had taken all of Barney's persuasive powers — plus £20 cash and a cheque for the outstanding balance of the rent — to mollify the landlord into sending away the workmen, two of whom Barney immediately recognised as freelance heavies from West Ham.

It was frustratingly ironical, thought Barney, that his cash-flow problems should come to a head just as he had found himself a well-paying case and was embarking at that moment on another. But this was typical of the unreasonableness of creditors: just when a man is doing his best to earn some money for them they disrupt his work by hounding him with phone calls, setting bailiffs on him, and locking him out of his office whenever his back is turned. And now he had to go out and concentrate on two difficult cases with the worry hanging over him that if he didn't get some money from Mr. Mundle before his cheque bounced he might well return to his office one day to find his desk, his filing cabinet and his padded swivel chair being carted off to be sold. If only Mr. Mundle and that other bloke had given him the advances he'd asked for; after all, it was the least they could do after giving him false names and addresses. Yes, that fact hadn't escaped him in the slightest; it was the first thing he'd checked on. He didn't particularly mind them doing that — in fact, he thought it a reasonable precaution — but he could see how it might possibly put him in a fairly tricky position with regard to being paid.

Barney reckoned it was probably no more than fifteen miles to the docks from his office in Clapham, but he didn't see any point in taking the normal route through Camberwell and Greenwich because that would take the best part of an hour and since the ship had docked over ninety minutes ago he needed to get there quicker than that. So he decided to take a shortcut.

At 7:05 p.m. Barney set off in his 62 Riley to meet a black man disguised as a sailor coming off the SS Von Speer, and from the London docks to take him to a flat just north of St. Pancras station which had been described by the tall man in the hat, Mr. Underwood, as a 'safe house'.

At 8:30 p.m. Barney was whistling 'Blow the Man Down' as he searched Hackney for any major road that would take him south to Greenwich or south west to Woolwich. He had, in fact, been badly let down by the

45

compass he'd installed ten years ago on top of the dash, which he would certainly have to take a serious look at. Then there was of course London's notorious shortcoming in adequately signposting streets. And if the man in the hat, the so-called Mr. Underwood, asked for his £15 back: well, he'd just have to regret to inform him that deposits are nonreturnable and he, Cecil Fitzalan, senior partner of Fitzalan and Huggins, privat detectives, can not possibly be held responsible for directional singularities and other unforseen circumstances.

At 9:10 p.m. he felt reasonably certain that if he took the Caledonian Road south from Islington he would arrive at the Bunch of Grapes in time for a good drink with the boys. It was somehow fitting, he felt, that he would pass within half a mile of the 'safe house' near St. Pancras station.

At 11:30 p.m., after a very good drink with his cronies and after failing to persuade his current girlfriend, Harriet, to see him home, Barney opened the iron gate that led to his basement flat in Clapham.

Access to Barney's flat, or as he liked to call it, his apartments, required the successful traverse of fifteen steps, a descent that owing to his chronic inability to remember to step down as soon as he opened the gate, Barney often made in a most precipitous fashion. And it was of a piece with his preceding run of misfortune that tonight would be another occasion on which he would fail to pay that first step the attention it merited and would consequently experience a slight difficulty in maintaining his equilibrium.

Barney fell down the steps.

This fact was noted by (a) a dog which announced or celebrated his fall by a round of loud staccato barking,

46

(b) the elderly lady upstairs who disliked Barney because he was a show-off and who considered that when Barney did occasionally come a cropper on the steps he was merely trying to draw attention to himself, and (c) John Madrid, who having failed to lure the Irish detective to a deserted pier was now standing in the darkness with the intention of roughing up Barney to make him talk and then, most probably, cutting his throat.

As far as Barney was concerned, the fact that he had fallen down the steps was noted only momentarily by him, for he now lay unconscious outside his door, his hat obscuring one of the lenses of his hornrimmed spectacles, and the light from the elderly lady's flat reflecting off the other.

As he gazed at the dark prone figure below him, it was clear to Madrid that this nosey private eye, the so-called Cecil Fitzalan, was in no shape at the moment to give out any information. Seeing there was no mileage in beating up on a zapped drunk, he decided to let him be for a day or two. Besides, he had an idea he could make use of this Huggins.

Madrid relit his pipe, then looked up at Lisa, who was sitting on the couch opposite him.

'I tell you, the guy's not playing with a full deck. Sitting there in this dive of an office with a lopsided moustache stuck on his face. Giving me winks and knowing smiles and coming out with stuff like "No job too confidential, that's our motto." And then this Cecil Fitzalan business. What did he hope to gain from that?'

Lisa said: 'Who is this Fitzalan?'

'I dunno. Might be nobody. This kook might have made him up.'

Lisa sipped at her coffee.

'But why would he do that?' she asked. 'From what you say, he hasn't attempted this deceit with anyone else. Don't you find that significant?'

'You think he's trying to pull something?'

'If you mean, is he playing a game with us, the answer is yes. First he makes himself conspicuous in the street outside, which means he wanted me to know I am being watched. Then he puts on this strange act for you in his office . . . By the way, was he sober? Any drugs?'

'Hard to tell with him, but I didn't smell any booze. I don't think he's a junkie. I've seen enough of them to know.'

She gave a caustic smile.

'Yes, you have, haven't you?'

Madrid glared at her. She said:

'You know, Johnny, I don't think we should underestimate this man.'

'I never underestimate anybody,' said Madrid, his eyes still on her.

'I'm glad to hear it.' She pulled a long filtered cigarette from the packet on the coffee table in front of her. Madrid reached over with his lighter. She said:

'At least he was too clever to be caught last night in your little trap.'

'Put it down to animal instinct.'

'Really?' she said with a lift of her pencilled eyebrows. 'Is that all it takes to foil your methods?'

Madrid reached for his cup.

'I think you're trying to needle me.'

A smile quivered on her thin red lips.

48

'Not at all, Johnny, I would have to take you downstairs for that.'

'Huh. That'll be the day. I guess you'd enjoy it though, wouldn't you?'

'I'd enjoy the irony of it, yes. But I suspect that in general I take less pleasure from my work than you do from yours.'

He said calmly: 'So I'm some kind of psycho, that the way of it?'

'No, you're not, Johnny. But you are a very sombre man. Why do you take everything I say to heart?'

Madrid shrugged.

'Look, about this guy last night. I had to get him somewhere really out of the way — London's a pretty crowded place and I wanted him to stay unfound till this thing was well over.' He permitted himself a rare smile. 'And the river's one of the best spots I know of for dumping unwanted customers.'

'That's better, Johnny.'

'Anyway, it came to me last night when I was outside his flat that this guy could be more use to us alive than dead. Despite what you say, I'm a hundred percent certain he doesn't connect me with you — I've made sure nobody has seen me enter this house — and I don't think he's anywhere near as smart as you seem to think. So I'm planning on using him. He's a natural for it.'

'A fall-guy, you mean?'

'Sure. I'll set him up so well it'll be like giving the cops a Christmas box wrapped up in tinsel paper and a bow.'

'How would you do that?'

'No problem. Send him out on some pretext to shadow the next mark, get him to handle the gun or whatever I'll be using, leave it for the cops to find.'

She frowned.

'But wouldn't the police think that too obvious?'

'No, if it looks plausible they'll jump at it. They're too busy to do otherwise. Listen, I read once of this guy who wanted to kill his girlfriend's husband, so he set it up so that everything would point to himself and then after he shot him he did a whole bunch of things that no killer in his right mind would do. He did them deliberately. But his plan didn't work, because you can't make things *too* obvious for the cops. To them it was just plain obvious; the subtlety was wasted on them. They arrested him and got a conviction.'

'Yes, but the police didn't arrest those men who confessed to the killings of the Yorkshire ripper.'

'That's different. They come out of the woodwork to confess to something famous like that. It would make the cops look stupid if they sent for trial some old bum who starts gabbling about cutting up broads in Whitechapel and making his escape in a Hansom cab. Particularly if the killings don't stop. Besides, Huggins won't be confessing to anything. It'll be the cops who catch our detective pal, right on the scene.'

'I'm still not sure why you want a fall-guy for this one. You've never needed one before.'

'You want Huggins out of circulation, don't you? Okay, if we do it this way the cops close their files on him and also the broad who's next in line for the chop. But if I knock off Huggins, that means two more investigations by the cops, which just possibly may lead to me. It's unlikely that all my cover-ups will fool them. Suicides are particularly difficult to set up.'

'They're much less fun too, aren't they?' said Lisa, grinding out her cigarette.

★   ★   ★   ★   ★   ★

At 3:50 p.m. on May 21, forty two minutes after John Madrid had slipped unseen from Lisa's apartments by the back door, a much less shadowy figure wearing a grey raincoat and with a hat pulled over his eyes embarked on the second phase of his undercover investigation by walking confidently up to the front door and pressing the bell.

Although reasonably sure that the second phase would go every bit as well as the first, Barney had in fact taken steps to prepare himself for any contingency that would require an immediate transition into the third phase — namely, tough tactics. There was in Barney's book an important distinction to be made between the third phase of the sub-group undercover investigation and the six phases of the two sub-groups that composed the penultimate group — namely, Tough Tactics.

Barney's book differed from most manuals of detection in the disproportionate amount of space given to bullying women, duffing up geezers, and intimidation in general. His main reason for according undercover investigation a mere sub-grouping (while Browbeating, for example, had a whole group to itself) was that he considered it time-consuming and generally ineffective, i.e. he wasn't very good at it. Direct action, however, was his forte. He had been a boxer, a soldier, a student of jiu jitsu, and had been on the receiving end of more threats and intimidation than probably anyone in Clapham. If he didn't know every dirty trick there was going, then he was always willing to learn. Barney wasn't one of those middle-aged men who fail to keep abreast of developments in their own field.

Standing outside Lisa's apartments, Barney awaited a different kind of development, one that he hoped would not require the implementation of the third phase. But if it did: well, he was now in possession of an imitation Luger automatic and he wasn't afraid to use it. He was also in possession of a splitting headache, but it would take more than that to stop Barney from continuing the investigation and at the same time going to bed with a high class callgirl, both at Mr. Mundle's expense.

The maid opened the door.

'Yers?'

'I've come to see the lady.'

'Ave yoo made an appointmint?'

'I have indeed.'

'Come in then.'

He followed her into a small sitting room that contained a piano and a smell of cats.

'Wait here,' she said and waddled off down the hall.

Barney sat down and waited. There was nothing for him to pry into in this room, but he decided to check the piano out anyway. He briefly considered making a sortie into the upstairs rooms, but he didn't want to risk blowing his cover quite so soon.

The maid came back.

'This way.'

He followed her into a dimly-lit room at the back of the house.

'She won't be long,' said the maid, closing the door after her.

Barney looked around. He had been in two rooms now and neither of them possessed a bed. There was a lot of strange-looking stuff in this one, Barney decided. Crosses, pulleys, straps, handcuffs ... It occurred to him that something had gone wrong. He'd been lured into a trap. Almost certainly that door was now locked. There were four henchmen lurking in the hall. They were going to give him the works. Mundle had set him up. He was in one of his tightest spots ever. He should have known better. The first phase had been just too easy. He'd got carried away. He had to pull himself together. He had to remember his tough tactics.

There was the sound of a step and in the five seconds it took for the door to open Barney decided (a) to agree to anything they wanted, (b) offer his services as a member of their gang, (c) declare he was Inspector Fitzalan of the Yard and inform them the house was surrounded, and (d) enter immediately into the third phase of his undercover investigation.

As the negligee-clad Lisa was completing her usual dramatic entrance, Barney was stepping out from behind an eight foot tall rack, pointing a dummy Luger automatic in her general direction and hissing between his false teeth:

'This is your last chance, sister. Do as I say.'

Closing the door with his foot, he added:

'Where's the rest of them? Yes, I'm wise to you. Do as I say.'

Lisa, whose first impression had been that the unknown visitor was a prominent lawyer who occasionally asked her to be a Bonnie to his Clyde now recognised the hissing man before her as none other than the mysterious B.H. Huggins. She looked frightened. She said:

'There is no need for a gun.'

Barney waved his pistol at her.

'That's for me to decide.' He pushed her into the room. 'I said, where's the rest of them?'

'What rest of them?'

'I said —'

'Please. I'll give you what you want. Is it money you

53

are looking for? I have plenty of that.'

Barney's response was almost automatic. Keeping his eye on the door, he said vaguely:

'How much are we talking about?'

'I'm not sure. I'll have to see what I have. But it is a lot.'

He said: 'I'm not holding you up, you know.'

'Then what are you doing?'

'I mean, you don't *have* to give me any money.'

She looked up from the pistol, held close to him, now pointing at her stomach. In the dim light of the lamp their eyes met, brown on glassy blue. He added:

'But it's okay if you do.'

She said earnestly: 'Have you done this sort of thing before?'

He felt awkward, wrong footed. He thought he'd told her he wasn't a stick-up man. For a moment he wondered if he might be undercover as a stick-up man. But if that was the case he wouldn't have told her he wasn't one. It was strange the turns this case had taken. He hoped that this particular one wasn't leading to a courtroom in which a bewigged judge was solemnly handing him down ten years for armed robbery. He decided he would have to watch himself.

'I'm not really threatening you with this gun,' he said.

She stared at him, waiting for him to continue. He said:

'I came here for a bit . . . you know . . . of the other.'

'I don't do that with strange men.'

He gestured at her equipment.

'So I see. I had the wrong idea about that stuff at first.'

'Perhaps. But that still does not explain your

behaviour. You came here to rob me, didn't you?'

'Nonsense.' Barney decided it was time to break off the investigation. He waved the pistol at her and stepped back. 'I'm leaving now and you'd better not try and stop me.'

'Don't be silly. You came here to steal my money and that's what you must do. Always finish what you start.' She stepped towards him. Barney retreated. 'How much do you want to steal?'

'I've told you —'

'But I insist. You must have something for your trouble.'

Barney considered the situation for a few seconds. He didn't want to do anything he might regret later.

'All right,' he said. 'As long as you're not leaving yourself short. Just a loan, mind you.'

She smiled.

'I think there's some over here.'

He followed her over to a tall cupboard against the far wall. Looking down at her breasts as she rummaged in the cupboard, he didn't notice the sole of her high-heel pressing on a button by the skirting board. When the door opened, Barney slewed round, Luger in hand. He caught a glimpse of the maid before Lisa hit him with an iron bar on the back of the head.

Barney's skull was quite used to that sort of treatment, so Lisa and the maid barely had time to attach him hand and foot to an X-shaped cross before he opened his eyes, glanced around him, tested his bindings, glared at them for several moments, and said in a voice loaded with disgust:

'Pair of bitches.'

Lisa said: 'Leave him to me,' and the maid waddled out, closing the door with an ominous click.

Lisa applied her slender finger to another button and Barney was cut off in the middle of another scurrility, 'I'll kick your poxy cu —' as the cross gave a jerk and started to move slowly in an anti-clockwise direction.

Barney's efforts to marshal his powers of reasoning, already damaged by two recent blows to the dome and a severe hangover, were further hindered by the sudden rush of blood to his head that occurred as he approached the half way point in his cycle. During the three minutes it took for Barney to make two orbits around his stomach, his stream of consciousness, expressed vocally only when he was in a reasonably upright position, resembled one of the darkest, most esoteric passages of *Finnegans Wake*. He was babbling mentally about the genuine Egyptian who stole Big Max's amusement arcade when Lisa stopped the cross and said:

'Ready to talk, Huggins?'

Barney's glasses had fallen off, but he could just about make out two seemingly enormous thighs towering up to a large black triangle. As he opened his mouth to speak, his teeth assumed that grotesque shape peculiar to people in upside down positions. He said with difficulty:

'I'm damned sure I am.'

'Excellent.' Another touch on the button and Barney was restored to an upright, more detective-like position. She said sharply:

'Why were you watching me?'

'A bloke who called himself Mundle told me to.'

'Describe him.'

'He's short and fat with a la de da voice.'

'What reason did he give?'

'Said you were blackmailing him.'

'Did he say why?'

'Said you were going to tell his wife he was sleeping with you.'

She snorted.

'I'd have to be asleep to lie in the same bed with him. What were you supposed to find out?'

'Something he could use to stop you blackmailing him.'

'And did you?'

'No. Drew a complete blank.'

She reached out and Barney embarked on another revolution.

'And did you?' she repeated when the cross stopped, her finger poised once more over the button.

'Nothing in the slightest,' he choked out. 'I've told you everything.'

She smiled.

'Some detective, you are. Do you always betray your clients' interests so easily?'

'But look what you were doing to me,' Barney spluttered.

'Oh, don't be a sissy! That was nothing. I have many men who ask for things much more severe than that.'

'Yes, but I have high blood pressure. I could have died on this thing. I don't mind the odd bang on the nut, but I had an open-heart surgery and the doctor was dumbfounded. He said I was a walking miracle. He —'

'I am not interested in your operations. I am going to release you now and you will leave this building in a quiet, sensible manner. You will await my instructions. Is that clear?'

'I'm working for you now?'

'You are.'

'My normal rates?'

'Don't be ridiculous,' she said, giving a sharp tug to the first of his bindings.

Barney picked up his hat and glasses and looked around for any change that may have fallen out.

'I can give you a special rate —'

'Get out of here!'

'I was going anyway,' said Barney and walked stiffly out of the room.

Lisa opened the cupboard and removed the Luger automatic, handling it with respect. Holding it under the lamp, she examined it closely. She began to laugh.

At that moment Barney was chuckling silently to himself as he marched down the sunlit street to his car. He had suspected there was more to this set-up than met the eye, and now, at his first attempt, he had uncovered the most valuable fact of them all.

In the seven days since Milton Wilmar had provided Lisa with a photocopy of another secret document, he had gone about his daily affairs in such an unsettled manner that both his wife and personal assistant had enquired if there was anything troubling him. Diane, his p.a., asked if there was anything at all she could do for him, and wondered if he wasn't having trouble with his wife, whom she had met and instantly disliked. Laura, his wife, asked him why he was either mooching around the house or staring at the wall like a half-wit, and wondered if he wasn't having an affair with his p.a., whom she rightly suspected of having designs on him. Both were unaware of the designs that were occasionally left on him by a dark-haired woman in a Kensington back room.

In the eight days since Wilmar had commissioned

B.H. Huggins to make enquiries on his behalf, he had made three exasperating phone calls to the detective, each time being fobbed off with an assertion that everything was under control.

So, on the morning of May 22, Wilmar arrived unannounced at the office of B.H. Huggins, opened the door marked PRIVAT DETECTIVE, and said:

'I hope you don't mind me dropping in like this.'

'Not at all, Mr. Mundle,' said Barney, who was swivelling thoughtfully in his chair. 'I was hoping you'd call. I have in fact some important information for you. Information that came to me only after extensive hard work that resulted in a major breakthrough.' He regarded Wilmar with a steely glint. 'A breakthrough that would have been made earlier if my client had not withheld significant facts from me at the start.'

Wilmar, who had occupied the chair by the hat stand, lowered his eyes. He was almost afraid to ask.

'What facts?' he said.

'We are both familiar with the facts as we know them. I see no point in discussing them, Mr. Mundle; or should I say' — Wilmar cringed under Barney's knowing smirk — 'Mr. ....?'

'I'm sorry. But you understand —'

'I understand a lot of things, Mr. Mundle.'

Barney leant back in his chair and rolled a pencil between his hands. Wilmar said:

'You mentioned a breakthrough.'

'That is correct.'

They stared at each other. Wilmar said with a touch of sarcasm:

'May I be permitted to know what it is?'

Barney responded in the same tone.

'I'm sure it's only an oversight on your part, Mr.

Mundle, but you haven't as yet come across with any deposit or payment.'

Wilmar had £300 in his pocket. He hadn't proposed giving Barney more than £100 of that, but it was now clear that the balance of power had shifted. He said:

'I intended to settle my account with you today. What is it now?'

Barney put his pencil to work.

'Seven days at £50 equals £350. Plus £115 expenses. Total: £465.' He smiled. 'I assume you want to pay cash.'

Wilmar looked doubtful.

'That's a sizeable amount.'

'Not for a man in your position.' The detective leaned forward aggressively. 'Of course, if you don't want to pay I will have to put the information to another use.'

Wilmar swallowed hard. He said with alacrity:

'I told you I intended to settle my account. It's just that —'

'It's just that you can't lay your hands on the money at the moment, I know. I'm sorry, Mr. Mundle, but you've no legal right to the information now and you've only yourself to blame.'

Wilmar pulled out his wallet and threw a wad of twenty-pound notes onto the desk.

'There! Three hundred pounds. The balance later today.' He watched anxiously as Barney removed the elastic band and started to count in a fast, fluent manner.

'Only £280 here,' Barney said gravely, pushing the notes back across the desk and fixing him with a reproachful glare.

Wilmar's chubby hands moved quickly through the wad. There was a twenty-pound note missing. He was almost sure Huggins had palmed it, but there was nothing he could do about it now. He said:

'You're right. The bank clerk must have made a mistake. I didn't mean to cheat you.'

Barney gathered in the money.

'Don't worry about it. You can settle with me later. Before three o'clock, that is. I make it £185. Right? Tens and twenties will do. I'd give you a breakdown on the expenses, but they were mostly undercover, so I can't. It would mean revealing my methods. That okay? It's normal practice.'

'Yes, of course.'

'Fine.' Barney snapped open his cigarette case and placed a handrolled in his mouth. After striking the match and lighting the cigarette in one movement, he extinguished the flame with a burst of smoke through his nostrils. He smiled at Wilmar.

'Want one?'

'Thank you, no. I prefer my own.' He produced his packet of Players, lighting up in a jerky, more pedestrian manner. He said:

'Please tell me what you have found out, Mr. Huggins.'

Barney settled back in his padded chair.

'You know, Mr. Mundle, one of the things a detective always has to be asking himself is: What am I assuming? And when I asked myself that in connection with your blackmailing the answer I got was: I am assuming that Mr. Mundle has been paying money to this Lisa woman, because that, after all, is what most blackmailers want, isn't it?'

Wilmar nodded glumly. He wondered how many detectives there were in London, and why out of all of those he had to choose this awful man.

'But that's not what this particular one wanted, was it, Mr. Mundle?'

'No.'

'No, it wasn't. And what was it she wanted?'

'I can't say.'

'Yes, you can say. I want to hear you say. Right here and now. What was it, Mr. Mundle?'

Wilmar stared at the smoke rising from his cigarette. Why, he wondered, was he allowing himself to be bullied by this man? Especially after just paying him three hundred pounds. Surely Huggins hadn't forced or tricked Lisa into telling him about the documents. That was most unlikely. But he obviously knew something. What was it? His real identity? That was even more unlikely. Whatever it was, he had to find out. He would feed Huggins a little of the truth, draw him out.

'I said, what was it, Mr. Mundle?'

'If you must know, I was required to deliver several documents.'

'Instead of money?'

'Yes.'

'What kind of documents?' asked Barney.

'They were of an historical nature.'

'Something to do with Germans?'

He caught his breath. 'How —'

'Something to do with German gold?'

Wilmar stared at him.

'Is that what you've found out?'

'It is.'

The senior civil servant ground out his cigarette. So that was it! The bitch was using him to uncover a hoard of Nazi gold. He might have known it would be something like this.

'Mr. Huggins,' he said, smiling tentatively, 'you have a very peculiar way of informing your clients of the results of your investigations.'

MAY 26   HAMBURG

As his plane approached Hamburg's international airport, Milton Wilmar was sitting at a window in the first class section rereading his own copies of the three documents he had delivered to the dark-haired whore in Kensington.

All were dated 1945 and were concerned with a 'certain incident' that occurred in the western sector of Hamburg. Actually, they were so infuriatingly vague that Wilmar couldn't see why they had been classified as secret in the first place. Some damn fool of a second lieutenant in the Birmingham Fusiliers had got himself in a jam, was sent home under escort, and then immediately dismissed from the service. It was all so hush hush that none of the three reports — from the military police to Battalion HQ to Brigade HQ to the

War Office — even mentioned the exact nature of the crime. Wilmar thought it significant that the young officer had not been court martialled; he could only infer from that that the offence, if publicised, would have had political repercussions. And still might have, he thought, considering his own position in this affair. Particularly if, as he had reason to suspect, a large quantity of gold was involved.

The No Smoking lights came on; the plane with a perceptible bump, reduced altitude. Wilmar replaced the documents in the inside pocket of his jacket, then looked down at the milling Autobahn and the rows of neat brown houses. As the moment for action drew nearer he attempted once more to examine his motives; but he was still unable to express clearly — or to admit to himself — his prime reason for coming to Germany all these years after a 'certain incident' had taken place. He wasn't even sure that he was in fact going to follow up on this gold business at all. He decided to play it by ear.

He passed through Customs without incident.

'Haben Sie etwas zu verzollen?'

'Nein, nichts.' No, he had nothing to declare — except, of course, three secret Government documents, but he didn't see any reason why German Customs should be permitted to pry into those.

He waited for a taxi.

'Fahren sie mich bitte zum Hotel Danzig,' he directed, climbing into a black BMW.

As they entered a ramp leading to the Autobahn the driver said:

'You are English?'

'Yes.'

'You are in vacation?'

'Both pleasure and business.'

64

They drove without speaking for a few minutes. The driver said:

'You are new to Hamburg?'

'Yes, it's my first time.'

'You know, I can show you round real good. I know all the real good places.' He chuckled. 'And I do not mean *das Museum.*'

Wilmar looked out of the window, thinking. Apart from a number of learned sentences, his German was far from fluent. It would be useful to have a guide who spoke English, awkward and Americanised though it may be. He said:

'All right. Can you meet me outside the hotel at nine tomorrow morning?'

'Sure, that will be swell all right.'

They turned off the Autobahn and went along a straight wide street lined with small factories and warehouses. Within fifteen minutes they were in the inner city.

Shortly after 9 p.m. Wilmar emerged from the hotel. He had showered, changed into a lightweight grey suit, and consumed, with the aid of a half bottle of *Liebfraumilch,* a hefty serving of roast pork and spiced dumplings. He was now in a mood to take in some local colour, and since he might never be in Hamburg again it would be a pity to leave without visiting the famous Reeperbahn, the red-light street in the district of St. Pauli.

Not, of course, that he would risk sampling the wares — he was more of an up-market type, and besides, he was in enough trouble with that sort of thing as it was — but the shady, self-destructive side of life had always held a fascination for him and there was certainly no harm in looking.

65

After five schnapps and a Dortmund export beer, and with Bavarian *Biermusik* ringing in his ears, Wilmar stepped out of the smoke-filled pub to resume his tour of the Reeperbahn. He hadn't meant to stay in the pub at all — just a peek and then on to something else — but the throbbing music, the general lack of inhibition, and particularly the waitresses with their miniscule skirts and suspenders had drawn him to a corner table where he drank and soaked up the atmosphere. Much less reserved than my lot, he thought, picking his way along the crowded neon-lit street. And that was only a pub. They'll be much more explicit in a night club, I'll be bound.

Once, when he had been forced to travel on London's Underground, he had taken a very dim view of the two young men wearing mascara and bright coloured shoes who had sat opposite him and talked to each other in light, drawling voices. But now he was even able to summon a smile for the youth with bleached hair who caught his eye and pursed his lipsticked mouth at him.

And when he saw at an intersection a midget, no more than two feet high, propped up on crutches, her shining brown hair touching the ground, he immediately stopped and put five marks in her tin.

'*Danke,*' she said, and the sorrowful look in her beautiful blue eyes stayed with him until he reached the next block and his senses were assailed by the lascivious front of the Black Angel Club.

After paying his fifteen marks admittance charge he descended into a large blue-lit cellar over which the tobacco smoke hung like a sheet. Rock music came loudly, but not painfully, from speakers set on the walls. A transparent screen had been placed across the stage, behind which three very female figures gyrated to the

66

music. Their faces were made up in a grotesque manner, emphasising ghoul-like eyes and sunken cheeks. Their nipples were large and painted black; their voluminous pubic hair was shaped to resemble respectively a heart, a penis, a question mark. They kissed each other, appeared to penetrate each other with their fingers, and rubbed themselves against the screen. When the music stopped they skipped out to the front of the stage, holding hands and singing what seemed to be a German nursery rhyme.

It was quite well done, thought Wilmar, picking up his cigarette that had burned untouched in the ashtray. He finished off his schnapps and ordered another. He was definitely getting into the swing of things now.

'*Sind Sie Deutscher?*'

He looked up at the dark-haired woman who had approached the table. '*Ich bin Englander,*' he said.

'Do you want a girl?' she asked in heavily-accented English, sitting down beside him.

He felt a little flustered. This was sudden. No standing on ceremonies here. 'You mean . . . you?'

'*Ja.*' Her tone said, And why not?

Indeed, Wilmar asked himself, and why not? She wasn't an awful lot younger than he was himself, but she was as voluptuous as they come. She was fairly bursting out of that see-through blouse; he could see the heavy stitching on her pointed bra. He said:

'All right. My hotel is quite near.'

The waiter came with his drink. She picked it up and drank it. She smiled at him, showing uneven gold-filled teeth. She said:

'That is *gut.* Come, we will go now.'

He nodded and got to his feet, taking care not to lurch over the table. He followed her out.

He waited until they were in the hotel corridor before mentioning his special requirements.

She smiled.

'Don't look so anxious. I never thought you wanted an ordinary screw. Very few of my men are wanting that. It will cost one hundred and twenty marks,' she added.

'That is for how long?' Wilmar had little experience of this class of whore; he didn't want to be cheated.

'I can not say. It depends on you, doesn't it darling?'

Wilmar rather doubted that, but he knew what she meant. He opened the door and preceded her into the well-furnished room.

She waited until he had undressed, then she unbuttoned her blouse, placing it over the headboard of the bed. She stepped out of her burgundy skirt and Wilmar wasn't pleased about the brevity of her briefs; little more than G strings they were, while he liked the trappings to be somewhat more substantial. At least she wasn't wearing tights; he quite liked these nylons with the elasticated tops that came up to about mid thigh. But he was disappointed with the size of her spare tyre; it was almost as big as his own. He definitely didn't like the look of that rash which spread down her neck to the strap of her bra. And what kind of woman, he wondered, would have a butterfly tattooed on the left cheek of her backside?

Wilmar caught a whiff of sweat from her armpits as she walked past him and pulled the leather belt from his trousers, which were hanging over a chair.

As Wilmar woke up, the memory of the previous night came flooding back to him. He felt dirty, sore and

68

hungover. It had needed half of the bottle of whiskey, sent up by room service after she'd gone, to blot out his depression and put him to sleep. He wouldn't have minded so much if he'd achieved a proper orgasm, but it was one of those times when the ejaculation is launched on the wrong beat and the pleasure is muted, almost nil. His head throbbing, he reached for the phone and ordered a pot of coffee, scrambled eggs, and a tab of aspirins. Then he slouched into the bathroom and had another shower.

He felt reasonably better after his breakfast. He lit a cigarette then spread the three documents on the bed. It was 8:25, so he had to hurry and formulate his plan for the day. Each of the reports mentioned this family called Tantau who had lived on the Wannseestrasse. The repetition of their names indicated that they were centrally involved in the 'certain incident'. There were five of them — Claus, Helga, Karen, Marlene and Sonya. In 1945 their ages ranged from seven to fifty, so it was unlikely that they were all still alive. It was possible, even probable, that the house they lived in no longer existed. Perhaps the younger women had married and changed their names. What kind of records did the authorities keep in the last year of the Third Reich? Had they survived? Were they available to the public?

It was a strange, formidable task, but he had known that before he started. Maybe that was the main reason he hadn't totally committed himself to it. When he had first heard about the gold in London he congratulated himself on twisting the situation to his own advantage; from a prospect of continuing blackmail or scandal to one of substantial wealth. He would certainly need more than his present reserves, a measly quarter million, if the police decided to raid Lisa's and discovered her file on

69

him. He would be out in the cold for a long time after that.

Yet this quest for gold seemed improbable, like something out of a film. Could that Huggins be believed? He had sounded plausible enough, seemed to know about the three reports, gave details of Lisa's plan to sell the gold in Argentina. Perhaps all good detectives were eccentric, Huggins just a little more than most. He was unscrupulous too. Despite the detective's hints, Wilmar was sure he hadn't found out his real identity; he would certainly have asked for more money if he had. Being in Lisa's power was bad enough, but the repercussions of Huggins finding out just didn't bear thinking about.

There was a telephone directory in the drawer of the bedside table. He looked up Tantau. There were six entries, none of them on Wannseestrasse. He decided to check that street out first anyway. It was now 8:55, so he put on his jacket and went down to see if the driver had arrived.

Number 112 Wannseestrasse, a three-storeyed terrace house, was obviously constructed well before the war. He rang the bell. His driver, whose name was Willy, stood beside him, ready to help out with a translation. When there was no answer he asked Willy to enquire next door.

'No good luck here,' said Willy after a short conversation with a middle-aged man. 'They have been living here for twenty years and they say no Tantau live there.'

'Who does live in that house?'

'Frammler, he said. Man and wife. Been around since 1951.'

'Where are they now?'

'Vienna. Coming back next month.'

70

'All right,' said Wilmar. 'Let's go on to the next one.'

By 3:30 they had visited the six addresses listed in the directory. None of the people interviewed had lived on the Wannseestrasse, nor had they heard of any family called Tantau who had. He paid off the driver outside the hotel and took the lift up to his room. Tomorrow he would check the records of the departments responsible for rates and property taxes. Right now he wanted a drink.

Closing the door he glimpsed a long shape against the wall. Before he could even turn his head he was grabbed by the lapels and thrown across the room. His back hit the carpeted floor. As he tried to rise he was grabbed once more and cuffed several times on the face. He fell back, stunned. When no more blows came he looked up and focused on a tall blond man, who said:

'What are you doing in Hamburg?'

Wilmar's mouth opened, moving silently. John Madrid knelt down, caught him by the throat and backhanded him until his cheek was bleeding from the impact of Madrid's gold ring. He said:

'I asked you a question, Wilmar.'

Wilmar spluttered: 'Who are you? What —'

Madrid hit him again.

'I'm going to keep on doing this till you answer me. I said, what are you doing in Hamburg?'

'I'm on official business. I —'

The hand crashed down again. Madrid said:

'I know about Huggins. So try again.'

Wilmar's face was a red pulp by the time he had told Madrid everything. His eyes were so swollen he could hardly see. His teeth were loose and the blood from his lips and tongue filled his mouth, ran down his chin. The first touch of the length of nylon on his neck was soft,

71

like a kiss. Then Madrid crossed his hands and pulled with all his strength.

After pushing the body under the bed and hanging a Do Not Disturb sign on the door knob, Madrid left the hotel by the fire escape. He was going to the airport, but since he knew that taxi drivers are required by law in most cities to list the times and locations of all their pick-ups and drop-offs, he decided to wait until he was well away from the hotel before hailing a cab.

Sitting in one of the airport bars, he read over the three reports he had taken from Wilmar. Replacing them in his pocket, he took out his pipe, filled it with his mild tobacco and lit up. He sipped at the vodka and fresh orange juice. He checked once more that there was not the slightest trace of blood on the front of his clothes. His hand was sore but there was no sign of damage. He hadn't, as he thought, grazed it on Wilmar's teeth. That could be dangerous, he'd read; a human bite can spread more diseases than a dog's.

One of his rare smiles spread over his face as he played with the idea of icing that high-class hooker in Kensington. Maybe he'd cut her up on one of her own racks, make out it was one of those creeps that did it. That would be ironic enough for Lisa, he thought, remembering her fondness for the word. There was no doubt she had it coming. She shouldn't have bull-shitted him about why she wanted all those people knocked off. She should have played it straight with him because he was doing something practically no other hit man in the western world would even consider doing for less than a quarter million, if at all.

As he left the bar to catch his flight to London he was already making plans for his return to Hamburg. If anybody could locate these Tantaus, he could.

MAY 29   LONDON

Barney Huggins hoped that he'd heard the last of Mr.
Mundle. It really wasn't his fault if the stout little man
went off on a tangent because of information received;
particularly if the information in question had been
given in good faith. Indeed, Barney wasn't at all sure
that the gen he'd obtained from Petesy Marker down at
the Bunch of Grapes should be in question; after all, he'd
never proved Petesy wrong yet. Admittedly, he'd never
set out to do that, but what was the point of hiring a
bloke for legwork and the more mundane undercover
activities if you had to check everything he did?

Barney considered himself fortunate to have found
Petesy. A detective always needed his sources, and when
you needed the latest on the Clapham and Fulham
underworlds, who better to ask than a chap like Petesy

who has more form than the paddock on Derby day. According to the standing joke down at the Bunch of Grapes, the down at heel Petesy was a perfect Lonely to Barney's wildly imperfect Callan. (Barney's attempts to recruit female agents 'of the right frame of mind' had been so unsuccessful that he was reduced to standing outside Holloway women's prison, which was how he met Harriet, his current girl friend.)

Apart from Petesy's reliability in the past, the reason why Barney could claim to have passed on that information about Lisa in good faith was simply that after thinking about it for several days he came to believe it himself. This, however, meant little, since after a requisite number of repetitions he usually ended up thoroughly believing his own lies, particularly the boasts.

And now, one week after Mr. Mundle's last visit, he had reached the point where he was planning to go after the gold himself. Or more precisely, he was thinking of planning to go after it. He couldn't go yet because he didn't have the money to travel to Germany. But even if he had, he still had to stay here and follow up on that important fact which he discovered on that only superficially ill-fated sortie into Lisa's establishment.

He had thought that her affluent clients would be only too happy to offer him a well-paid post as a security consultant charged with ensuring that their sex lives remain nobody's business but their own, which was how it should be; but he hadn't realised how much they needed his services, how vulnerable they were to improper manipulation, until he went in there and discovered the exact nature of their sexual adventures.

Barney was sitting at his desk working out a fair and

reasonable fee structure when the door opened and the so-called Mr. Underwood stepped in.

'How's it going, Mr. Underwood?'

'Okay.' Madrid sat down on the chair by the hat stand.

'Good. That's the stuff. Hot day, isn't it? So sticky yesterday I had to shave off my moustache. Now about the other night —'

'Yeah, I'm sorry about that. The ship didn't dock until yesterday. I got the wrong date from the shipping line.'

Barney's tensions eased.

'I must have waited hours for that bloody boat. Standing there in the cold, with not a sinner about, waiting and watching, and the sorrowful thing about it was that I checked myself before I went and they said it wasn't due in till yesterday. But I thought that since this was of a political nature the ship was coming in unofficial like, and my whole worry was that it had gone to the wrong pier and I'd missed it. And I didn't have your phone number, don't forget. Of course, I knew better than to go to the safe house . . .'

Madrid wasn't even listening. After he filled and lit his pipe, he took seven ten-pound notes from his wallet and placed them on the desk; an action which brought Barney's monologue to an abrupt end.

Madrid said: 'That'll cover what I owe you plus a forty pound advance for the next assignment.'

Barney pocketed the money, saying:

'I think I may be able to fit you in, Mr. Underwood. Though things are a bit hectic at the moment, what with Mr. Huggins still away on his case and one or two people wanting missing persons found. But I'll see what I can do. Now who do you want me to meet this time?'

76

'Nobody. I want you to follow somebody, a woman. I want you to keep her under constant surveillance for two days, note down where she goes, who she sees, who visits her. This must be done very discreetly. Nobody, especially not her, must be aware of your presence. Think you can handle that?'

'No sweat. Following is one of my special fortes.'

'I'm glad to hear it. You want to take down the details?'

As Madrid was leaving he paused at the door and said:

'By the way, you ever been to Canada?'

Barney wondered what this was leading to.

'In a manner of speaking,' he said cautiously.

'What do you mean?'

'Well, in 1950 I arrived in Halifax by boat, but there was an outbreak of smallpox on board, so they refused to let us land and we came back to England. I think it was smallpox. Could have been diptheria.'

Madrid nodded and went out.

Barney was pondering the significance of that question when he looked up to see Petesy Marker standing silently just inside the door. Barney was displeased. This was contrary to instructions. He snapped:

'What are you doing here?'

Petesy sidled over to the desk. Barney noticed with irritation the oil stains on his checked suit. Petesy said:

'Sorry, Mr. 'Uggins, but that bloke who was just in here, I've seen him before.'

'Where have you seen him?'

'He sees that Lisa woman.'

'A punter, you mean?'

'No, he's more than that.'

'Sit down,' Barney said. Feeling slightly repentant for having snapped at him, he clicked open his silver case and offered him one of his misshapen cigarettes.

Angela Cambridge grabbed the phone and with a shaking hand dialled 999. When the duty sergeant came on the line she shouted hysterically:

'A man tried to kill me! I've been shot! There's a body here in my living room!'

Until two weeks ago, Angela, a twenty-six year old mother of two, had led a normal uneventful life in the surburbia of north Barnet. The first crack in her structured existence came with the totally unexpected suicide of her mother, Mary. For two days after that Angela lay heavily sedated in a darkened bedroom of her detached house. Yesterday she had gone out shopping for the first time since the tragedy. Her outing was a success; she was able to deal with the people she met in a calm, rational manner. She felt that she was over the worst.

Then all the progress she had made was shattered by a tall blond man walking with a gun in his hand into her living room. The sight of the long black silencer had made her senses swim; the look in his pale eyes sent her heart throbbing in her throat. As he had stepped slowly towards her he seemed to smile. His mouth opened and although his words reverberated in her mind she couldn't seem to grasp their meaning. He was still moving towards her and still talking; it was like a dream in which she was striking out at someone with arms that had the strength of a feather; but she couldn't even move her mouth let alone her arms. Her terror reached its climax as the man stood still before her and slowly raised the gun.

She screamed. There was a muffled crack, she was flung back by a massive jolt to the shoulder, and as she fell to the floor she caught a glimpse of another man slamming a metal bar onto the back of the tall man's head.

She felt the other man's hands on her shoulder. She heard him say: 'You'll be all right. He's only winged you.' She didn't resist as he gently lifted her into a chair. She felt another surge of terror when he said: 'You better call the cops before he comes round. Don't touch the gun unless you see him stir.'

The other man knelt down by the tall man and went through his pockets. Then he stood up, pushed back the spectacles on his battered, lined nose, and walked smartly out.

When the maid opened the door Barney pushed past her, saying:

'Get her out here quick. This is urgent.'

'Ooh, I can't —'

Barney grabbed her by the wrist, pulling her in front of him.

'Move, you big dollop of lard. I said this was urgent.' He gave a shove to help her down the hall.

He lit a cigarette and waited. He felt determined. The first jackpot of this difficult case was almost within reach. He looked at the flattened knuckles of his right fist, then pressed them against the wall. He was giving her one more minute to get out here, then he was going in.

'What do you want?' said Lisa, appearing at the end

of the hall. She was wearing her long black negligee. She looked irritated. Barney just smiled. He said:

'You're in big trouble.'

He opened the door of the waiting room that contained a piano and a smell of cats. Lisa followed him in. She said:

'I told you —'

Barney said: 'Shut up and listen. Your boyfriend who calls himself Underwood tried to set me up for a fall-guy. He had me following this woman before he went in and shot her. He was going to leave my calling card on the floor. But I played him for the dope instead. I cracked his skull with an iron bar and left him for the cops.' Barney dropped his butt to the carpet and ground it out. 'I think that leaves you in one hell of a jam, lady.'

Lisa was looking scared.

'I do not know any Underwood.'

'Don't you? Tall bloke with blond hair, wears fawn suits? Smokes a pipe? Comes in here regular but isn't one of your customers?... Just shot Mrs. Cambridge?'

She was breathing heavily.

'I tell you I don't know this man.'

Barney turned to the door. He sighed.

'That's her story and she's sticking to it ...'

'Wait. What are you going to do?'

'What do you care? You just tell the cops you don't know any Underwood, they'll believe you. Just be sure to hitch up your skirt and bat your false eyelashes when you say it ... Jesus, lady, don't you know when you're in a spot?'

'Are you going to the police?'

'I've got to. I've got to tell them everything. If I don't, they can still nail me for an accessory to murder.'

'Why did you come here?' she said.

Grabbing her arm, he pulled her to him until their lips almost met. He whispered:

'To give you a chance of persuading me not to go to the cops. Unless I'm far wrong, your pal's a professional hit man. That means he won't shop you. Or if he does, it won't be until he's convinced he's made the best bargain with the law. That gives you time to leave the country. With a racket like yours you can start up anywhere, all you need is a passport. But you can't go unless I let you. You can't even leave this house unless I let you. Have I made myself clear?'

'How much do you want?' she said viciously.

Barney released her arm.

'I worked it out that you gross around a hundred grand a year. I'd be vastly surprised if you paid tax on that, so it's likely you don't put it all in the bank. I reckoned that until you launder it through some scheme or other it's kept in a deposit box. Am I right?'

She stared at him, her face expressionless. He said:

'Look, I'm in two minds about this. You start haggling or denying you've got money and I'm going to lift up the phone.' His mouth twisted in a smile. 'Before you get sent down for the big one you better put all your cash where it'll gather interest.'

'All right,' she said wearily. 'I will give you all that I can manage.'

'How much would that be?'

'Almost thirty thousands.'

'Pounds?'

'Yes, pounds, damn you.'

'Don't get upset, it's only a matter of *quid pro quo.* You don't like it because this time you're on the wrong end of the transaction.' He looked at his watch. 'It's just after two. We'd better get cracking before the banks close.'

As they were leaving the house Barney said:

'By the way, there wasn't anything to this gold business, was there?'

'I don't know what you mean.'

Barney shrugged.

'Nah, I didn't think there was.'

JUNE 2   HALFIELD

Catherine Deauville waited until Tim's wife was out of the room then said:

'I don't know what's the matter with you, Tim. You've become so withdrawn and sullen these past few months. I can't even talk to you anymore.'

Abruptly, he put down his glass and got to his feet.

'Don't talk rot,' he said, walking to the window. He ran his fingers down the venetian blinds then turned, saying: 'Look, I'm as concerned about my family as the next man, but I have neither the time nor the inclination to embroil myself in this matter.'

'A matter?' she cried. 'Is that what you call it when two of your family are dead and another one is nearly murdered? For God's sake don't be so stupid.'

'Keep your voice down,' he hissed. He went over to

her chair, stood before her. 'So I'm withdrawn, sullen and now stupid. Oh yes, and it wasn't too long ago you called me callous. Do you really think you have the right to talk to me like that?'

She sighed heavily.

'Tim, at the moment I'm not too worried about your finer feelings. I'm trying, without much success it seems, to get across to you the seriousness of this situation. Why can't you accept that what's happened is not a series of coincidences?'

He sat down and finished off his drink.

'Why,' he asked as if to himself, 'do women always have to view things in such personal terms? They seem to think the whole world revolves around their families, they have no sense of perspective —'

'That's both untrue and irrelevant,' snapped Catherine, 'and you know it.'

'Listen, will you? What I'm saying is that there are billions of people in this world and that means there's an almost infinite number of combinations or occurrences that can take place between them. What may appear to you to be an impossible coincidence is not only possible but is almost certain to happen somewhere and sometime. In this instance it has happened to this family and we must accept that.'

Catherine said sharply: 'Do you really believe that? That's almost as bad as predestination.'

Tim was losing his patience.

'Don't be absurd. It's nothing whatsoever to do with that.' He got up quickly and went over to the drinks cabinet. 'What the hell do you expect me to do, Catherine? Are you suggesting that I put on my deerstalker hat and investigate a sex killing in Toronto, a suicide in Luton, and an attempted murder, if that's what it was, in Barnet?'

Catherine waited until he returned with his gin.

'No, I don't,' she said, looking at him levelly. 'I simply expect you to tell me why all this is happening.'

Tim glared at her as if she had slapped his face. At length he said:

'That's a ridiculous thing to say.'

'Is it?' With sharp movements she opened her handbag and lit a cigarette. 'Then why is it you've been acting as though you had something to hide? Do you think that after all these years I don't know you?'

'Something to hide?' he repeated. 'Are you implying —'

'No,' she said quickly. 'I'm not suggesting that you're involved in this —'

'Then what the hell are you suggesting?'

'I'm just saying that I think you know more about this than you admit.'

He was still angry.

'Yes! Exactly! You've just phrased the same bloody accusation in different words. If I didn't stab my own daughter to death or put the rope around my sister's neck then I know who did or I know why it was done. It was all part of my sinister, murderous plan, wasn't it?'

She held up her hand.

'Please, Tim, don't say things like that. You know that's not what I meant.'

'Get out of here,' he shouted. 'You won't talk to me like that again.'

They both looked round as the door opened. Tim's wife said:

'Is everything all right?'

He jumped to his feet.

85

'No, it's not all right. I want this bitch out of here.'
He went past her into the hall. Seconds later they heard
the door slam.

Catherine's eyes were loaded with tears. She said
softly:

'Tim's a very troubled man.'

Tim parked in the yard of the Calbury Scrap Iron Co.
When he went into the prefabricated hut that served as
an office, Calton looked up from his desk and said sourly:

'You know it's not a good idea for you to be seen
here.'

Tim sat down on a metal chair with a misshapen
cushion on the seat.

'I suppose I could say it's not a good idea for you to
get yourself arrested.' He brushed dust from the back of
his trousers.

Calton sat hunched over his desk, twirling a pencil
in his hand.

'That's nothing to do with you.'

'Really?' Tim smiled thinly. 'Perhaps you'll be good
enough to explain why it hasn't.'

'Didn't you hear why I was pulled in?'

'I heard something, but not from you. You've been
a difficult man to contact this past week or two.'

'I've had to spend a lot of time in Birmingham
— on business.'

There was a pause. Tim sat motionless, looking at
him. Calton continued to twirl the pencil. There was the
sound of a lorry rumbling into the yard. Calton said:

'What was it you heard?'

'Just tell me what happened.'

86

Calton put down the pencil and lit a cigarette, blowing out noisily. Looking at his coarse, scarred features Tim wondered if Wendy found him physically attractive. He assumed she was still seeing him. It had been on the point of his tongue several times to tell her what he'd heard that night when the policemen came, but she was being so sweet to him lately he didn't see any reason for bringing it up. He was even wavering on his unspoken decision not to buy her the car.

Calton said: 'They thought I broke into the steel works.'

Tim had heard about the break-in. It seemed they were after the platinum stored in reinforced wire cages. The security guard came up on them after they had triggered the silent alarm, but they escaped through a hole in the perimeter fence and he was unable to identify any of them.

'I gathered that much. Were you involved?'

'Of course not. What do you take me for?'

'Then what made the police think you were one of them?'

'That's what I'd like to know.'

'Look, Calton,' said Tim angrily, 'that's not good enough. You must have some idea.'

Calton returned the glare.

'I've been cross-examined enough by the cops without you bleeding well starting too. Get the hell out of here before I lose my temper.'

Tim got up and stood in front of the desk.

'That's not all, Calton. You owe me money.'

'You'll get it through the normal channels,' Calton snapped.

'It seems these normal channels aren't operating too well lately. The last payment is three weeks overdue.'

'I said you'll get it.'

'You received a cheque from the steel works over a month ago. I should have been paid from that. What have you done with my money? Tell me, Calton, before I . . .'

Calton stood up. 'Before you what?' The two men faced each other. Tim's fists clenched at his sides. Calton stood rigid, the cords bulging in his neck. 'Well?'

Tim's face was strained, his breath came fast and heavy. He thought: This is ridiculous, like two boys squaring up for a fight. As he looked away Calton gave a snarl of contempt, 'Get out. I'll see to you later,' and pushed him away from the desk.

Tim reacted instantly. He was aware only of an overpowering rage against the hated Calton. As he sprang forward Calton caught him with a short punch to the top of the head. His consciousness flickered for a moment, then he parried instinctively another punch and grabbed Calton by the lapels of his coat. Jerking him forward, he thrust his knee with all his force into the man's groin. Calton made a sharp choking sound, his hands reaching out spasmodically for Tim's eyes. Tim thrust his head downward and sent his knee once more into Calton's groin. Then he brought his fist up in a vicious uppercut and there was the sound of teeth breaking as it connected with the underside of the man's jaw. Calton's hands jerked up to his face as he fell forward onto the floor.

Tim stood back, still white with anger.

'See how much you enjoy Wendy now,' he shouted.

He went out. By the time he reached his car he was trembling so much he could hardly fit the key into the ignition.

★ ★ ★ ★ ★ ★

Tim spent the rest of the afternoon in the balcony of an almost deserted cinema, watching reruns of *Duel at Diabolo* and *The Molly Maguires*, and sipping from a half bottle of scotch he'd bought at an off-licence. He had just wanted a dark place where he could unwind with the whisky and be alone, and he watched thoughtlessly the adventures and misfortunes of men engaged in the wars of the Old West and the Pennsylvania coal mines.

It was drizzling when he left the cinema. He drove along Halfield High Street and then north a few blocks to Wendy's flat. This was his evening for seeing her. The possibility that Calton had phoned her weighed heavily on him as he went up in the lift and opened the door.

'Hello darling,' she said, giving him a quick kiss. 'Bit of rain, I see.'

He sighed with relief.

'Mmm, I like that skirt. New one, is it?'

She struck a suggestive pose, hands on hips, emphasising the slit that came half way up her thigh.

'Bought it today. Not too Susie Wongish, you think?'

'Not at all. Anything goes well with your figure.'

'Oh, you sweet-talking old devil you,' she said, affecting a provocative sway of the hips as she went into the kitchen.

He was preparing two drinks at the liquor cabinet when she came out with a bottle of Beaujolais.

'Bought it to go with the steaks. I suppose we should open it soon.'

He was about to say it was much too early, then he remembered his resolution to stop being fussy about things that didn't really matter.

'Good idea,' he said. 'I shall have to take it easy with these before dinner or I'll be in no state to enjoy it.'

She wagged her finger in a mock scolding.

'Yes, I could smell it. You can see it in your eyes, too. Didn't you go to work today?'

'No, I took the day off. Here,' he reached her a gin and lime. 'I hope that's the way you like it.'

After a time he stopped worrying that the phone was going to ring. They had dinner about nine. He said it was the best steak he'd ever had. She smiled and said that was one compliment she couldn't believe.

When she went to the bathroom to clean her teeth he carried out their plates to the kitchen. As he was scraping the remains into the garbage pail under the sink, he noticed a pair of her nylon briefs on top of the basket of dirty washing. Impulsively he reached for them and brought them to his face. For a few moments he breathed in her aroma; then fearful that she would see him and laugh at him, he went to put them back. His hand stopped as he noticed the other pair that had been under hers. He picked them up and held them out. An extra-large pair of men's Y-fronts, white with blue vertical stripes. God help him, they weren't even Calton's!

He heard her coming out of the bathroom. He walked into the living room, holding the men's briefs behind his back. She said:

'Shall we play records? I bought a . . .' She broke off as she saw his face. 'What's wrong with you?'

He went up to her and held the briefs in front of her face.

'I assume these aren't yours.'

He could see her thinking, making up lies. She said curtly:

'I'm helping the woman next door with her washing. She's not well.'

'What number?'

She turned away. He put his hand on her arm.

'Why don't you answer me?'

She flared round.

'Answer you? What you mean is, answer to you.'

'How can you say that? I don't interfere in your life at all.'

'Don't you? What the hell do you think you're doing now?'

'I asked you a simple question. I'm entitled to know . . .'

'You're not entitled to search my home for clues that I'm sleeping with other men.'

He said weakly: 'Well, aren't you?'

She looked at him with loathing; he'd seen contempt in her eyes before but never this. She brought her face close to his, her breasts rose and strained against the cotton blouse, her cheeks were flushed, her eyes narrowed.

'Yes,' she spat. 'I am. Did you really think you were enough to satisfy me? You didn't even come near. Not once. Not a single time. I need real men, not pests who creep about asking questions about dirty underwear.'

His mind went blank. He was conscious only of her glaring eyes and the smell of the toothpaste she'd been using. Then, with an almost physical sensation, a surge of hatred coursed through him. His hand swept up to the side of her face. As she reeled back, wide eyed, from the blow, he grabbed the front of her blouse with both hands and tore it in two. A button hit him gently on the neck. He struck her again, a slap that lost its impact as her head went back. He grabbed her hair, pulling her forward, gripped her blouse at the back and wrenched and tore, forcing her arms back where the material refused to rip.

Releasing her hair, he grasped the strap of her bra and tried to break the clasp.

Her head jerked up, loosening his grip on the strap. With a snarl she brought her hands up behind him, digging her nails into his back, clawing at his thin shirt, moaning, gasping.

He reached for the waist of her skirt, tearing at it until the buttons snapped off. He wrenched the skirt down then grabbed her arms and threw her onto the settee. She lay face down, sobbing, the skirt tangled about her feet. He clutched her hair again, pulling her head back; he forced his other hand under her crotch, gripping it as hard as he could. As she started to scream he banged her face into the cushion. He ran his hand along her stomach to her right breast, then grasped the other, squeezing until she cried out. Getting to his feet, he tore down her briefs then grabbed her legs and heaved her so that she lay over the arm of the settee.

'Ram me,' she whimpered. 'Ram me now!'

JUNE 10   LONDON

Wendy took a taxi from Euston station to the Dinmount Hotel in Hampstead. She was wearing a grey woollen suit, a white cotton blouse and a maroon scarf of French silk; her hair was fixed in a loose bun under a wide-brimmed hat. An outfit, both stylish and conservative, that was eminently suitable for a young woman meeting her well-to-do aunt.

Looking out at the shops, the clubs, the familiar parks and landmarks, the uniqueness that is London, Wendy hoped that she could persuade her aunt to let her leave the drabness of Halfield and return to the city life which she had missed so much. She hadn't, she supposed, been all that unhappy in Halfield — there had been no shortage of men, for instance, and after the first month she hadn't had to work anymore at that awful

93

department store — but she was used to living in London and that's where she wanted to be.

As arranged, her aunt was waiting for her in the hotel bar. Wendy couldn't see her at first, then she went along to an alcove not visible from the door and there she was, sitting in a dark blue suit and hat and smoking a cigarette. Wendy bent over and pressed her lips onto her black hair.

'*Wie geht es Ihnen, Lisa?*' she said, smiling.

'Well enough,' said Lisa in the same language, the same accent. 'Did you have a pleasant trip down?'

Wendy sat down opposite her.

'Not too bad. Is this for me?' She gestured at one of the two drinks on the table.

'Yes, I ordered it with my own. I think you like vodka.'

'Oh yes.' She took a large sip. 'Mmm, that's good after the journey ... So tell me, what's been happening?'

Lisa said softly: 'My man has been arrested.'

'You mean?'

'Yes, he bungled the last one. He just managed to wound her in the shoulder. The police caught him in her house.'

'God! That's not like him.'

Lisa gave a grim smile.

'He was unconscious at the time. Knocked out by the man whom he tried to frame for the killing. It was perfectly done. He led Madrid on, waiting until the crucial moment before taking him out, then he left before the police arrived.'

'But why did Madrid need to make use of this man?'

'That's what I asked. I pointed out that he had already been outmanoeuvred by this fellow, who is, after

94

all, a detective —'

'A detective? Madrid must have been out of his mind.'

'A private one. A strange, shabby private one, but still a detective. He outwitted me too.'

'There's more?'

'Yes: We initially regarded him as a threat. Then Madrid changed his mind; and after meeting him, so did I. I thought I had persuaded him to work for me. I was convinced he hadn't connected me with Madrid. But after getting rid of Madrid he came to me, he claimed Johnny had killed this woman, he said I was involved, he said he was going to have me arrested if I didn't pay him money. So I did. I gave him thirty thousand pounds.'

Wendy put down her drink. Wide-eyed, she mouthed the words thirty thousand.

'Oh, Lisa,' she said.

Lisa smiled.

'Don't look so shocked. The notes I gave the poor bugger were counterfeit.'

There was a pause as they gazed at each other, their eyes celebrating the wonder of it all. A titter, a chuckle, a spasm of the shoulders, then they were laughing heartily at the detective who didn't know dud money when he saw it.

'Lisa, Lisa, you're the trickiest woman I've ever heard of.'

'Mind you, they were very well made. Made in Germany, like all the best things.'

'Including you, my sweet aunt, including you.'

'You flatter me too much.' Lisa reached for her handbag. As she lit a cigarette her expression became more serious. 'Tell me about this Deauville,' she said, smoke streaming from her nostrils.

Wendy sighed.

'He is another strange man. I can't make him out at all.'

'Why is that, dear? Omitting, if you please, a character analysis.'

'He is very moody, unpredictable, violent.' Catching the look of pain in her aunt's eyes, she regretted her choice of words. 'You remember Calton?' she continued. 'Well, about a week ago Deauville went round to his yard and gave him an awful beating. This surprised me because I had thought Deauville would be afraid of him.'

'They were fighting over you?'

'I'm not sure Deauville knows about Calton. I think they were quarrelling over some racket they were involved in.'

Lisa was suddenly interested. She had always wondered how a clerk at a steel works could afford to keep Wendy.

'What was that?' she said.

'Calton told me about it one night when he'd been drinking. It's quite simple really, but it explains a lot of things. Once a week Calton delivers iron scrap to the steel works. The lorry is driven over a large scale set in the ground and the iron is weighed. Deauville's accomplice tampers with the scales so that the reading is two or three times as much as it should be. The scale ticket is sent to Deauville, who approves it, makes a fictitious entry in the inventory records, then it's sent on to the accountant for payment. Deauville gets half of the extra amount from Calton. That's it.'

Lisa raised her eyebrows in appreciation.

'Quite a nice little scheme.'

'I thought it wasn't bad. Of course, I knew Deauville was up to something and I suspected he was up to it with

Calton. But I couldn't get anything out of Deauville, so I used a little pressure to wheedle it out of the other one.'

Lisa said: 'I hope you were more successful in persuading Deauville to talk about an other matter.'

Wendy twisted her mouth.

'Yes and no. There's no doubt of course he's the same man who was mentioned in those reports, and he admits being in Hamburg in 1945. But he won't talk about what he did there.'

Lisa said grimly: 'You can hardly expect him to.'

'You still want me to stay with him?'

'Of course, it's more vital now than ever. This is precisely the time when he's most likely to move away, to go to some place where he's not known.'

'Oh, I should have told you,' Wendy said, suddenly remembering. 'Calton was hurt so bad by Deauville that he's going around threatening to take care of him. He's already told two people that I know of.'

Lisa gave a slow smile.

'That could be very convenient,' she said. 'In fact, it could be incredibly convenient.'

Since Barney Huggins didn't know the notes were counterfeit he proceeded to distribute them around London in a relaxed, nonchalant manner, and it was this more than anything else that allayed suspicion in the various pubs, clubs, hotels and bawdy houses he frequented, so that two weeks after he had accompanied Lisa to the safe deposit box Barney was still very much at large.

Even Petesy Marker didn't realise they weren't genuine; the thirty pounds Barney had given him hadn't stayed in his possession long enough to permit an examination. Barney, who had a soft spot for his down at heel assistant, would have liked to have given him more but he was sensible enough not to flash money around people among whom he was notorious for his insolvency. That was one mistake he wasn't going to make.

He had decided to give up active detective work for a while, moving out of his office and his apartments in Clapham, and with the indifference the wealthy often display towards bills presented by their inferiors he had neglected to pay the outstanding rents on both premises. He was now living in a private hotel near Victoria, and it was from there he set out on an overcast afternoon for the nearby pub where he was meeting Petesy Marker.

Petesy nodded his cap-covered head and reached for the pint of bitter. 'Ta, Mr. 'Uggins.'

'*Prosit,*' Barney said, pronouncing it to rhyme with Does it.'

'What's that again, Mr. 'Uggins?'

'It's German for Mud in your eye.'

'Oh.' He smiled. 'It's all knowledge with you, Mr. 'Uggins. No wonder they call you the Professor down at the Bunch.'

A smirk played briefly on Barney's creased face. He reached for his glass. After making substantial inroads into his pint of Guinness, he wiped his mouth with his hand and said:

'Let's have it then. What's Lisa up to now?'

'Precious little. Least it's a mystery to me what she's doing. 'Asn't left the hotel yet.'

'That you know of,' Barney qualified.

'That's right, Mr. 'Uggins. I do 'ave to knock off now and again. Catch a bit of kip, you know?'

This smacked to Barney of slacking off; he made a mental note to put Petesy under spot-check surveillance. He said:

'Has she had any visitors?'

The little man shrugged.

'I don't know if somebody goes up to her room. She keeps the curtains drawn all the time.'

'Well, has she talked to anyone in the lobby or the bar?'

'Dunno. They won't let me into the hotel.'

Barney cast a withering look at his assistant's shabby suit.

'Don't you have any other clothes? You've been wearing that suit since I've known you.'

'I do, but they're not as good as this what I've got on.'

What was to be done with him? Barney consulted the smoke-stained ceiling for inspiration. Yes, that was it. He'd rent a long dress coat and one of those false fronts they used to wear in the thirties, a triangle of shirt and bow tie. Perhaps a monocle. Or even two monocles.

'Did I say something funny, Mr. 'Uggins?'

Smiling, Barney reached for his wallet.

'No, I wasn't laughing at you, old son . . . Here's a quid, get us two more in.'

'You want me to put the rest, Mr. 'Uggins?'

Barney threw 20p onto the table. Ungrateful little wretch, he thought. He said:

'There you are, old son. Isn't the price of drink fierce these days?'

Petesy nodded sympathetically.

'Need to save up 'fore you go down the boozer nowadays. Bloody robbery, it is.'

While his assistant was getting the beer, Barney

99

wondered why the black-haired dominatrix hadn't left London as he'd told her to do. He hoped she wasn't plotting some form of revenge on him. That was a situation that would call for some real Tough Tactics. He might have to bring in the Kilburn mob, or even the Belfast ones. They'd learn her all right. He was glad that strange heavy of Lisa's was out of the way. A very nasty piece of work that Underwood was. It was a good job for him he'd sussed him early on. Talking of hard geezers, it was a pity the Old Bill had taken Big Max away. Barney was planning to invest some of the money in one of his book shops, before he spent it all. It was a particular pity that he paid off all his debts to Big Max just two days before he was lifted. Only goes to show, you never really know people. He wouldn't have thought counterfeiting was Big Max's style at all.

Catherine Deauville placed the empty sherry bottle next to the two glasses on the round tin tray that advertised Woodbine cigarettes. There was just room for the cups and plates of the light supper she had prepared for herself and her friend Doris. After depositing them on the table in the small kitchen of her ground floor flat in Holland Park, she returned to the living room and put on once more the Bach Double Violin Concerto. She sat down on the threadbare settee, which her parents had bought for her more than thirty-five years ago, and closed her eyes. Running her fingers over the filigreed woodwork at the front of the arm, she pondered what Doris had said about the attempt on the life of her niece Angela.

Her friend was almost certainly right. Angela's

description of her attacker was bound to be distorted. Probably, if she could persuade the police to let her see him, he would turn out to be quite different from the man she saw lighting his pipe that evening in Jarvis Street, Toronto. She hadn't had a good look at him, just a glance really, a moment's stillness of the binoculars before she continued to scan the street for a glimpse of her other niece, Cay.

Yet she had remembered him. There was something about him that had stayed with her, a feeling of some indefinable quality that hinted of violence, destruction. She seemed to remember that he was tall and blond, too. It was funny, Angela said, but even with the shock of this man appearing with a gun in his hand she noticed immediately that he was North American. It wasn't so much the cut of his suit but more the way he wore it, the style of his sleek blond hair . . .

That music's too loud, she thought. It's almost midnight. Those people above are in bed by now. As she rose from the settee there was an explosive crash of breaking glass. The petrol bomb smashed against the fireplace, sending a stream of burning liquid onto her head and chest. With her hands to her face, she stumbled about the burning room, banging into the standard lamp, tripping over the coffee table. She lay screaming on the carpet, making only spasmodic, instinctive attempts to smother her burning cotton dress, until the room became a furnace of flame and heavy black smoke.

JUNE 14   HALFIELD

'The phone's ringing,' Wendy said. When Tim didn't seem to hear, she pushed him away with one hand, gripping his hand that was moving up her thigh with the other. 'Let me answer the phone.' She stood up from the settee and smoothed down her dress. She went into the bedroom to the phone, closing the door.

'Are you alone?' Lisa asked, speaking in English.

'Yes. Deauville's in the next room, but he can't hear me. He's had seven gins since dinner so he's not his usual alert self anyway.'

'I have good news for you. You can go back to London.'

'Permanently? I mean —'

'Yes. You've finished with both Deauville and

Halfield. Do you have a lot of personal property in the flat?'

'Just clothes really, a few records and books. He bought the furniture.'

'I suggest you rent a large car for that. Choose a company that has branches in London.'

'Of course. When will I leave?'

'In two days. Visit me at the hotel on the sixteenth. Same time.'

'All right.'

'See you soon.'

Wendy put down the phone and went into the living room. Tim looked up through narrowed eyes. He said:

'You're looking pleased with yourself. Good news?'

'In a way.' She sat down beside him and patted his hand. 'It was only my aunt.'

'What did she want?' It was clear he didn't believe her.

'It really was my aunt, darling. She asked me to go down to London for a while to look after my grandmother, the poor soul's on her last legs now. I really should go, because if I don't I could quite easily find myself left out of her will.' She rubbed his hand in her own. 'And you don't want that to happen, do you darling?'

Tim didn't look over-anxious about the possibility of Wendy losing her legacy.

'How long will you be gone?'

'Oh, no more than three or four weeks.'

'But that's a month!'

'So it is.'

'You mean you're going to leave me here for all that time so's you can babysit some old bat who —'

'Now, now, darling, don't be churlish. It doesn't

103

become you.' She smiled derisively. 'You'll just have to make do with your wife, won't you?'

'That's another old bat.' Holding on to the arm of the settee, he got to his feet and went unsteadily to the cocktail cabinet. 'Don't s'pose you could ring that aunt of yours and tell her you're sick or something?'

'No, there's too much at stake. I have to go and that's that. Be reasonable, Tim.'

He put down the bottle, came over and stood before her, swaying gently.

'And what's that?' he demanded. 'Who's being reasonable? I can have something at stake too, you know.'

'If you can't talk sensibly —'

Lurching forward, he gripped her shoulder. She gasped in pain. He shouted:

'I said you're not going.'

Springing to her feet, she brought her hand up in a vicious swing, hitting him so hard on the jaw that he lost his balance and fell down, landing on his backside. His legs flew up and there was a thud as his head hit the carpet. She said:

'I wouldn't advise you to lose your temper with me tonight. I'm not able to go through that routine every week, you know.'

She helped him to his feet and walked him to the settee. He sat with his head on his chest, his eyes closed. She said:

'It's quite obvious you're in no state to drive home tonight. You can stay here, but only if you promise to behave.'

He sniffed, said nothing.

'Well, do you?' she snapped, and he nodded reluctantly several times.

104

'All right then,' she said. 'Go and clean your teeth and get into bed. I'll be in in a minute. Off you go now.'

Poor sod, she thought, watching him stagger into the kitchen. He doesn't even know where he's going.

Lisa arrived in Halfield by train in the afternoon of June 17. Petesy Marker, who had received a forty pounds advance from his employer, was on the same train. When Tim didn't show up in the downtown bar he frequented, Lisa checked into a small hotel not far from Wendy's flat.

After seeing his subject safely into the hotel, Petesy, with a bottle of South African sherry in his raincoat pocket, went off in search of somewhere to sleep. It was a mere moment's work to pick the lock on a caravan he found adjacent to a large unlit house on the outskirts of the town.

Barney would 'ave kicked that door in, he thought, pulling the curtains. He lit a carefully shielded match. Cor, it's ever so nice in here. Make a good gaff, this would. Petesy, who was chronically out of lodgings, toyed with the idea of stealing a car to transport the caravan to London. That would be a lark. Imagine the look on Barney's kisser if he spied me sailing down the Lavender Hill with this in tow.

He lay down on the narrow bed and opened the bottle, taking a long pull of the sweet, aromatic liquid. He sighed. Wish he'd say what this is all about. He groped in his pocket for a butt. Not that I'd believe a word he swore. Real flannel merchant, he is. It must be a marvellous world inside that bloke's head. Tell him about her buying a Gerry paper and a book on the gold market and he's off, shouting 'So that's it!' and making a mystery out of a bleeding molehill.

Even Harriet says I'm a proper mug for going along with him. He lit the butt quickly. So's she, come to that. Gawd, I'd love to been there when she saw that picture of herself, half starkers, in that sophisticated sex life magazine. Send ten quid for the rest, all poses, underwear extra. She must have wondered where all her drawers were going to. I dunno what kind of bloke would do that to his missus. Don't hold with that at all.

The next evening at the hotel, Lisa slid into the sleek black number she'd bought specially for Tim. She picked up her coat and her dark-spangled purse, cast a final glance into the mirror, then left the room and descended two flights of carpeted stairs to the lobby. A well-dressed man stared at her and said good evening. She walked straight past him into the darkening street.

Several people looked up as she entered the lounge bar, then carried on with their conversations. She stood at the door, frowning slightly, glancing around as if she were meeting a waiting friend. There was the sound of a juke box in the next bar; it was playing 'Walking the Floor Over You'. Her eyes stopped at a middle-aged man sitting alone at a table near the wall. He looked up and smiled at her. It wasn't him. She would know him from more than his photograph.

She moved slowly towards the bar. The music and the chatter grew louder. A man said archly, 'Ah now, that's another story.' A high-pitched voice called, 'Two scotches please, Captain.'

Then, suddenly, the noise seemed to die away as she saw the man sitting on a stool at the bar. She stood

motionless, staring at his back. His head moved slightly
to one side. As she caught his eyes in the bar mirror, her
breathing stopped and her head rang as if she had been
struck. Quickly she lowered her eyes and glanced round
for a seat. The sound of the room came back; she was
conscious of her heart throbbing; she felt unduly warm.
She lowered herself behind a table against the wall and
started to take long, slow breaths.

'For a moment there I thought we knew each other,'
said Tim, standing at the table.

'I thought so, too. But I must have been mistaken.'
She opened her purse. 'Would you mind —'

'No need for that,' he said smiling. 'What's your
tipple?'

'Really, I would rather —'

'Nonsense. Be a pleasure. C'mon, speak up.'

She looked doubtful for a moment, then apparently
relenting:

'If you insist. A vodka with tonic please.'

'Ice?' he asked, going to the bar.

'Please.'

She smiled weakly. It had been easier than she'd
expected. She opened her purse and lit a cigarette, then
sat back, inhaling deeply. As she watched him returning
with the drinks, his blotched features barely concealing
a smirk, she thought she would like to get this over with
as quickly as possible.

'Here we are then.' He sat down opposite her.
'Weren't meeting anyone were you?'

She glanced around the bar.

'I don't see my friend at all.'

'He or she?'

'A girl friend of mine. She must have been delayed.'

'That's all right then,' he said heartily. He raised his

glass. 'Here's health.'

'Yes,' she said and drank most of the vodka.

'My word, you must have been in need of that. Get you another?'

Lisa almost wished that he wasn't so anxious.

'Not just now, thank you.'

They had four more drinks, Tim becoming even more loquacious, rambling on about the lack of amenities in Halfield and making hackneyed jokes at which she forced herself to smile; Lisa saying little, deftly avoiding his personal questions. Returning with the next drink, he sat down beside her on the long padded seat, his leg touching hers. This was a relief to her; she had found it difficult to look him in the eyes.

After the barman stopped serving and people were leaving noisily, sombrely, several of the women engaged in animated chatter, some of the men with exaggerated straight backs, she reached for her purse and coat, saying:

'Thank you for the drinks. I'm glad I met you tonight.'

'Not at all, s'been my pleasure entirely.' He touched her arm. 'Look, don't get the wrong idea, but couldn't we pop round to my flat for a last one. It's just round the corner.'

She almost smiled at the trace of pleading that came through the upright, sincere manner he was trying to adopt.

'I really should be getting back. Some other time perhaps.'

'Just half an hour, I promise.'

'No, not tonight.'

'Tomorrow then. Will you meet me tomorrow?'

She seemed to consider the matter.

108

'Very well.'

'Same time?'

'I may be a little late.'

'I'll wait for you.'

She could see he doubted she would be there. She stood up, saying:

'We might go somewhere different tomorrow night.'

He caught the hint of promise.

'Whatever you like,' he said, smiling.

The barman called: 'Come on now, ladies and gentlemen.'

JUNE 20   LONDON

'Ta, Mr. 'Uggins.'

'Prosit,' Barney said with a trace of irritation. They were in the pub near Victoria and Barney wondered how they had fallen into this way of going, with him always having to buy the beer. He said:

'How do we know she won't scarper while you're down here, and then she'll be lost and we won't know where she is?'

Petesy was feeling a little irritated himself.

'That's a good point, that's a bleeding good point, that is. P'haps you could've thought of it before you sent me up there with a measly forty quid in me pocket.'

Barney's hornrimmed glasses twinkled with a steely glint. Petesy looked down at his feet and continued in a milder tone:

'You expect wonders of people, Mr. 'Uggins. I mean. even with kipping in a caravan and having one nosh a day you can't stretch forty quid for ever. I even had to thumb it back here.'

Stifling a caustic remark about too much boozing and not enough initiative, Barney decided to concentrate on the more central issues of the investigation.

'Who's this bloke she's been farting around with?'

'I've seen him but I don't know who he is. Has a black moustache and drives a blue Cortina.'

'That should narrow it down a lot,' Barney said sneeringly. Lowering the level of his pint by a good three inches, he regretted the sorrowful fact that his assistant, cheap though he may be, had neither the appearance nor the *savoir faire* to penetrate useful places like car registration authorities and apartment rental offices. Putting down his glass, he fixed the little man with a wide-eyed stare and said:

'I suppose you did all right. This isn't a straightforward investigation by any means.'

'I'd an idea it wasn't.'

'No, not by a long chalk.' He snapped open the silver cigarette case and offered it to his colleague. Petesy produced a single match from his breast pocket, igniting it on the tiled floor. 'That's why,' Barney continued, 'I have decided to take over myself.'

'Whatever you say, Mr. 'Uggins. Though I'm sure it needs doing.'

'You see,' Barney explained, blowing smoke at the ceiling, 'an investigation is like a game of chess. There's a time for the little pieces and there's a time for the big pieces. And when the little pieces find themselves in the box the big pieces like the rooks and knights and castles go after the biggest piece of all, which in this case is the black queen, and if they're smart enough they put her in the box too. Am I making myself clear?'

Petesy rubbed irritably at his stubbled jaw.

'I wish you'd mention what you mean. I dunno if I like being called a pawn.'

Barney, who hadn't intended to make himself that clear, smiled and said:

'Depends on the game, old son. It wouldn't be the first time a little piece has gone in and done a checkmate.' He jerked out his wallet. 'Here, get us a couple more.'

Petesy, whose feelings could be salved quite easily by the offer of a pint, nodded and said:

'All right, Mr. 'Uggins.'

Barney was swirling thoughtfully the last inch of stout in his glass when Petesy came back from the bar, plonked down two pints, and said in a low voice:

'From what I just heard, you're in a bloody different game of chess now, mate.'

Annoyed at his assistant's unseemly familiarity, Barney looked up, adjusted his glasses to get a better glare at him, curled his upper lip at the side and said:

'Explain yourself.'

Petesy bent over and whispered in his ear:

'Big Max's put a contract out on you. That means you're in shtuck mate ... Dead shtuck!'

JUNE 21   HALFIELD

Lisa was taking special care with her make-up this evening, the anniversary of her parents' wedding. Sitting at Wendy's mirror for over half an hour, she applied each cosmetic in an almost ritualistic manner, like a celebrant preparing for a great black ceremony, moving patiently towards the final metaphor, the mystery of her breath sighing warm and scented over the image of blood on her long perfect nails.

Tim was a very worried man as he left the steel works at 8:35 p.m. The auditors had returned unexpectedly two days ago. They were in there now, going through his records, comparing them with the scale tickets for the past two years. They said it was just a routine step they'd neglected on their recent audit. They said it without looking at him. They knew the lie was on their faces. He saw it there all yesterday and today. He saw the undercurrent of excitement in the way they worked, the expectation of a discovery, a kill. Above all, he knew the Fraud Squad detectives had visited Calton and had taken all his files away.

He turned right at the gates, towards the flat he could no longer afford. That dark-haired woman would be there. He'd given her the key last night when she offered to prepare a steak fondue for him. She even hinted at the possibility of greater intimacies after dinner. But Tim was no longer interested in that. He just wanted to get drunk.

By the power of positive thinking Barney had changed from a badly scared man into a desperate one. He had arrived in Halfield in his ancient Riley at 7:45 p.m. In the boot was a briefcase containing wads of crisp bank notes which he now knew were phoney but was going to spend anyway. He had called into a High Street pub and drunk six whiskies which were like a fuel to his fierceness. He was standing in the doorway of an apartment building across the street from the flat. As soon as the torrential rain eased off he was going in there to give that whoremaster the worst thumping of her life.

For once, his presence was so deftly concealed that it was noticed only by a man in a long leather coat who was also watching the flat.

★ ★ ★ ★ ★ ★

When she heard the door opening, Lisa was in the kitchen chopping two pounds of choice steak into small cubes. The table had been set, and the two sauces, wild herb and cranberry, were in glass bowls next to the dishes of mushrooms and green salad. A bottle of Burgundy sat open on the counter, beside it a half-filled glass and next to that a green marble ashtray with smoke coiling from a neglected cigarette.

Three men ran in from the rain. They came into the entrance, breathing heavily, a tall one shaking his hat, another patting his neck with a large handkerchief. The third one, oblivious to the water running down his face, stood with his hands in the pockets of his leather coat. His eyes were dark and hostile, and their stare was returned unwaveringly by a fourth man wearing a greatcoat and a wide-brimmed hat.

Barney flicked his butt at Calton's feet.

'You'll know me again,' he said tightly.

The tall man put on his hat and moved closer. A gust of wind swept into the entrance, propelling the cigarette with a trail of sparks against the door. Calton said:

'I know you're not a cop.'

'Bully for you.'

Calton turned his head slightly towards the tall man.

'All right, boys,' he said.

Barney placed his right foot against the wall at his back. As the two men stepped towards him he projected himself forward.

Impaling a cube of raw steak on the long fork, Lisa immersed it in the simmering fat. The fondue pan, with a small spirit burner underneath to keep the fat hot, sat on the table between them; to the side were dishes of sauce, salad, pineapple, mushrooms, and a bowl of crusty French bread. Waiting for the meat to cook, she poured the last of the first bottle of Burgundy into Tim's glass.

'You are in a bad form tonight, I think.'

He looked up from staring at his plate and ran his hand down a cheek now almost continually blotched from the effects of his drinking.

'I have a lot on my mind.' He forced a weak smile. 'But I mustn't let it interfere with my enjoyment of both a splendid meal and the company of a beautiful woman.'

Smiling at his compliment, she removed the fork from the fat and dipped the meat partially and briefly into the wild herb sauce. She said:

'I am glad you mentioned you have the equipment for this. I am so fond of it.'

'Yes, got a taste for it myself after I went to Switzerland one year. Ever been there?'

'No, but I believe it's very beautiful. The Swiss are clean and tidy, so they help keep it like that.'

He seemed amused at her banal sentiment.

'Not like us, eh?'

'Oh, I don't know,' she said off-handedly. 'They are a bit like that where I come from.'

He sipped at his wine.

'Where's that then? I'd an idea you weren't born in England.'

'Hamburg,' she said. 'Ever been there?'

★ ★ ★ ★ ★ ★

In the prefabricated hut of the Calbury Scrap Iron Co. Barney sat in the metal chair with the misshapen cushion and sneered his defiance at the three blurred figures before him.

'You're making a vast mistake if you think I'd talk to the likes of you.'

The tall man drew back and delivered a swingeing blow to the side of Barney's head; his spectacles, which had been hanging from one ear, finally fell off, dropping with an unpleasant clunk onto the linoleum floor.

'I'd seriously advise you not to step on those glasses,' Barney warned them.

'That's enough of that!' Calton cried, showing his exasperation. 'Who are you working for? Is it Deauville?'

When there was no answer, he nodded at the tall man, who stepped forward with a short punch to Barney's battered nose.

'Why did you come up from London? Did Wendy shop Deauville? Or did he shop me?'

Barney looked up one-eyed. Blood from where the tall man's ring had cut him earlier was running into his left eye. His mouth opened and closed several times, then he began to talk in an indistinct whisper.

Calton's second confederate growled: 'I'm not having any part of this. That geezer's going to croak if you carry on like that.'

'Shut up! I want to hear what he's saying.'

Barney continued to whisper.

She turned her face away from his hard, forceful mouth. His hand gripped her shoulder, pressing her to him with a fervour that surprised Lisa after his earlier lethargy.

She breathed in deeply through her mouth then said: 'The bed would be more comfortable than this.'

He kissed her again then, as if fearful her mood would change, got up from her and reached out his hand. Lisa's face was expressionless as he led her into the bedroom.

He left the door half open so that light could enter from the lamp in the living room. He kicked off his shoes and started to unbutton his shirt, then he stood motionless, watching as she pushed the straps of her woollen dress over her shoulders and with the grace of the truly sensual lowered it slowly to her feet. The skin of her upper thighs and stomach seemed very white in the semidarkness of the bedroom.

Detective-sergeant Jack Stewart of the Regional Fraud Squad picked up the file and let it drop onto the cluttered desk. He looked up at his colleague, Jim Munro, who was standing at the side of the desk, waiting for him to finish reading the reports that had just been sent in.

'You were right, Jim. It was them after all.' He looked at his watch. 'Ten to eleven. Think we should pick up these three birds now?'

'Better safe than sorry.' Munro put down his mug of lukewarm tea. 'I only hope they're not in bed. Always makes me feel like the KGB when we arrest people in their pyjamas.'

'Speak up, damn you,' Calton urged, bending over so that his ear was close to Barney's mouth. 'What's that?'

'These ones who shopped you . . .' Barney murmured.

'Yes? Yes?'

'. . . they were in it together.'

'What's their names?'

'This new bint Deauville's took up with, she's a professional grass. This firm down the Smoke sent me up to work her over.'

Calton's face was a mask of hatred.

'You mean this bastard Deauville's done a deal with the cops?' he shouted.

Barney nodded sorrowfully. The tall man shifted from foot to foot. Calton seemed to be thinking. The other one picked up Barney's glasses and handed them to him, saying:

'No hard feelings, mate. We don't want no strife with the London boys.'

'Let's go,' Calton said urgently. 'There's not a minute to lose.'

Watching Calton and his two heavies storm out with blood in their eyes, Barney thought it was just as well that he hadn't continued with his plan to draw the mouthy one close, punch him in the throat and then have a go at the other two. But he was still very mad about the whole thing, so he went out in the rain and threw house bricks through the windows of the hut and the two lorries in the yard.

'Oh God,' he murmured, 'that's sensational.'

Crouching down between his legs, she ran her tongue along the inside of his thigh, from his scrotum to the back of his knee. Then she repeated the process, moving in the opposite direction. He sighed again and reached out for her to get on top of him.

'That's it,' he breathed as she settled herself over his groin. She gripped his tumescence and guided it. He gasped. He stretched his body, thrusting upwards.

'Don't rush,' she smiled. 'It's nice and warm as it is.'

Bending over, she ran her hands down the sides of his face. She touched his ears, his nose and his eyes. Her fingers entered his mouth, along his tongue, between his teeth and lips. She could tell from his eyes that he liked it. She lowered herself a little more, until her nipples touched his chest. He sighed and closed his eyes.

With one movement she slid the blade of the knife into his mouth. He choked and jerked. Gripping his hair with her left hand, she moved forward onto his chest.

'One move and you are dead,' she hissed. He stared at her with wide, frightened eyes.

'I think the name Tantau means something to you,' she said, spitting the words at him. 'You remember? You remember that May night all those years ago? It was raining then also, wasn't it?' She paused, allowing him to visualise the scene. Her face was drawn, the skin over her cheek bones had tightened, giving her features an almost ghoulish quality. She continued slowly, instilling virulence into each word.

'It was warm so my mother left the window open when I went to bed and I lay listening to the rain. I heard your lorry draw up, the banging on the door, the loud voices — and then the shots. Who did you kill first, second lieutentant? Was it my father? Or did you begin with the women?'

Suddenly he brought his hands up and grabbed her hair. As she plunged the knife further into his mouth he gave a terrible, muted shriek. His body jerked violently.

120

She twisted the blade free and plunged again. With his hands on the bed he forced his trunk up, throwing her back.

The knife was still in his mouth. She scrambled off the bed and stood with her back against the wall, staring at him. Trickles of blood ran down his chin. He jerked the knife out and gazed at her with large, crazed eyes. As she made a tentative step towards the door, he lurched from the bed and stood with his forearm against the wall, blocking her escape. With the knife in his hand he stumbled towards her. She screamed. He reached out for her, his fingers touched her shoulder. She recoiled, still screaming, still staring at his bulging eyes. With a grotesque lunge he reached her, grabbing at her hair. They collapsed to the floor, the knife dropped from his hand. As his body convulsed on top of her, his mouth opened and blood poured over her face and breasts.

The door bell chimed.

Dispatching two other cars to pick up Calton and the third member of the gang, the operator of the scales, Stewart and Munro set out for Tim's house in the suburbs. After being told by his wife that he had not yet arrived home they proceeded to drive around Halfield in the hope of seeing him. Thorough as it was, their intelligence on this case did not include the fact that he frequented a certain flat near the town centre.

Driving along High Street they picked up a brown Zodiac and followed it until it stopped outside Wendy's flat. Stewart and Munro got out simultaneously, slamming the doors.

'Calton!'

Calton slewed round. The tall man stopped and stood still, the other one moved behind him. The policemen walked towards them through the rain.

'Wesley Thomas Calton, a warrant has been issued for your arrest.'

At this particular moment Calton was in no mood to let himself be arrested. As Stewart stepped closer he hit the policeman with his elbow on the cheek bone. Munro rushed at him, trying to grab him by the neck from behind. After a few moments hesitation the other two men came to the aid of their boss.

It wasn't until he got out of his Riley that Barney noticed the struggle outside the flat. Always one to enjoy watching a good street-fight, he walked quickly down to the five men and stood beside the Zodiac. Then, recognising the three hoods who had abducted him, he moved closer to the affray and waited for a suitable moment to get his own back.

He was after the tall man in particular, so when he saw him getting to his feet after being downed by Munro, Barney stepped smartly forward and kicked him in the face. That was so easy that he turned his attention to Calton himself and hit him with a perfect right hook behind the ear.

Stewart was so grateful for his assistance that he apologised for having to ask him his name and address and accepted without a murmur the unlikely-sounding Underwood Fitzalan, proprietor of the Blue-eyed Maiden pub in Belfast.

After the police and their three captives had departed, Barney bounded up the stairs to Wendy's flat and rang the bell. He rang it several times. He thumped on the door. He shouted, 'Open up in there, I am a detective.' He tried to pick the lock. He ran down the stairs to his car and came back with a jemmy. He forced the lock.

Standing in the bedroom doorway was a naked woman with crazed eyes and a knife in her hand and with blood dripping down her face and body; and when he saw that he ran down the stairs again, got into his car and drove straight back to Clapham.

FEBRUARY 26   HAMBURG

Snow was falling in Hamburg. The past week had seen several fierce blizzards, but the inhabitants of that city, with the unquenchable vitality of most Germans, had gone about their business and pleasure totally unhindered by the weather.

Inside Lisa's centrally-heated apartment it was a constant seventy degrees, a comfortable temperature in which to pursue an occupation that demanded a partial divestment of one's person. Sitting in her well appointed sitting room she lit a cigarette and lay back to relax after the last session, though that had entailed little that was physically tiring. It was an easy matter to sternly direct a person to scurry around with a brush and pan, shouting out warnings that the carpet must be absolutely spotless, and never of course showing the least satisfaction with the results of the labour.

Lisa's new maid liked that sort of client too, even if it happened to be, as in this case, a woman. Lisa smiled at the almost fetishistic obsession the German *Hausfrau* often displays towards her housekeeping duties, which, particularly among older women, tend to form the pivot of her existence.

Noticing that the maid had brought in her mail, she went over to the small table near the door and carried the six letters back to the settee. Five were clearly from prospective clients; the sixth, which she opened immediately, was postmarked London and bore Wendy's distinctive scrawl.

My dear aunt,

Before I tell you my news I must inform you of a rather peculiar and unfortunate development of which I was totally ignorant until this morning.

You recall that when I left the flat in Halfield I took with me my books. Inadvertently, I included among them one of his, and although I was aware of that as soon as I unpacked in London, it wasn't until yesterday that I had a look at it. The photocopy I include speaks for itself, but I should add that I rang the publishers this morning and was told that it was withdrawn from circulation last March. They wouldn't say why, but since it was only published last year it could hardly have been distributed at all. I would guess an injunction or D notice.

I bought a new car last week . . .

Lisa picked up the photocopy of closely printed text. The title, author and publisher were written in ink at the top of the page.

Another example of this occurred in Hamburg on May 1, 1945. In response to reports of resistance in the form of sporadic rifle fire, a six-man patrol entered a house in the west side of the city. While searching an upstairs room, the section commander, a young second lieutenant, heard shots being fired below. Going down to investigate, he found that one of his fusiliers had, without any apparent justification, killed four of the occupants, an elderly Lutheran minister and three women. Incensed by the man's brutality, the officer shot him dead with his pistol.

The secondary point to be made here is that it was his display of summary justice rather than his responsibility, as section commander, for the murder of civilians that excited the wrath of his superiors. It was, in fact, only the need to disavow responsibility for the crime, with its potential political reverberations, that prevented the young officer from being much more severely dealt with than he actually was.

Lisa let the paper fall to the plush carpet. It occurred to her that she had made a mistake.